Sprinkles and Secrets

ALSO BY LISA SCHROEDER

It's Raining Cupcakes

I Heart You, You Haunt Me

Far from You

Chasing Brooklyn

The Day Before

Sprinkles and Secrets

by LISA SCHROEDER

Aladdin

NEW YORK   LONDON   TORONTO   SYDNEY

ALADDIN

An imprint of Simon & Schuster Children's Publishing Division
1230 Avenue of the Americas, New York, NY 10020
First Aladdin hardcover edition September 2011
For information about special discounts for bulk purchases,
please contact Simon & Schuster Special Sales at
1-866-506-1949 or business@simonandschuster.com.
The Simon & Schuster Speakers Bureau can bring authors to your live event.
For more information or to book an event contact the Simon & Schuster
Speakers Bureau at 1-866-248-3049 or visit our website at www.simonspeakers.com.
Designed by Karin Paprocki
The text of this book was set in MrsEaves.
Manufactured in the United States of America 0811 FFG
2 4 6 8 10 9 7 5 3 1
Library of Congress Cataloging-in-Publication Data
Schroeder, Lisa.
Sprinkles and secrets / by Lisa Schroeder. — 1st Aladdin hardcover ed.
p. cm.
Companion book to: It's Raining Cupcakes.
Summary: Twelve-year-old Sophie is excited to have the opportunity to audition
for a television commercial until she learns the company is Beatrice's Brownies,
the biggest competitor to her best friend's family's cupcake shop.
Includes recipes for chocolate treats.
ISBN 978-1-4424-2263-6 (hardcover : alk. paper)
[1. Best friends—Fiction. 2. Friendship—Fiction. 3. Bakers and bakeries—Fiction.
4. Auditions—Fiction.] I. Title.
PZ7.S3818Sp 2011
[Fic]—dc22
2010048277
ISBN 978-1-4424-2265-0 (eBook)

For my dear friend, Lisa—
I had so much fun remembering our magical afternoon
together watching WICKED *as I wrote this book.*
I have, indeed, been changed for good.

Sprinkles and Secrets

Chapter 1

chocolate ice cream

THE ULTIMATE COMFORT FOOD

J think there are two kinds of happiness.

There's the real kind of happiness when you *have* to smile because you feel so good inside. It's like you've just eaten the most delicious cupcake or cuddled with the most adorable kitten. When you look around, everything looks like it's trimmed in gold. Beautiful. Joyful. Happy.

Then there's the fake kind of happiness. Something is supposed to make you happy. Your brain keeps saying *you should be* happy *about this* and you want to be, but no matter how hard you try to feel the real happiness, for some reason you can't. So you smile anyway and put on the best happy show you can because you don't want to look like a bad person. Sometimes, though, if you're lucky, the fake happiness eventually and magically turns into real happiness.

Today I'm supposed to feel happy and excited. Instead I feel sad and jealous. No one knows that, though. I made sure of it. All day at school I was the picture of happiness. I should get an Emmy for my performance today. Or an Oscar. Or, at the very least, a new tube of lip gloss, because my lips are really dry from all that smiling.

As I ride my yellow mountain bike home, my legs pumping hard and fast and my face all scrunched up and ugly because I don't have to pretend to be happy anymore, I think of that horrible old woman, Miss Gulch, from *The Wizard of Oz*. The one who took Toto from Dorothy? I probably look like her. What a scary thought.

I take a deep breath, slow down my sad and jealous legs, and tell myself to relax. And then I turn my thoughts to the list of things I go to when I'm in serious need of cheering up. Well, not an actual list. That might be weird to have a piece of paper with *Sophie's List of Pick-Me-Ups* written at the top and then a list of items that fill the page.

Usually I'm a pretty happy person. But there are some days, like today, when the world feels like a big, rotten tomato. (For the record, I hate tomatoes.)

I go over my mental pick-me-up list and realize that with the long, boring weekend stretching out ahead of me, I'm going to need almost every single thing on the list to help me through it.

First on the list is my dog. Daisy is a Havanese, which means she's an adorable, white bundle of fluffiness. And before you think I'm really shallow and only love my dog because of how she looks, when I say she's cute, I mean even her personality is cute! When she wags her tail, which is a lot of the time, her whole body wiggles. She has a small collection of stuffed animals (ones I used to play with) that she's claimed as hers, and she loves it when I grab one and throw it so she can chase it and bring it back to me to play tug-of-war. And when I've worn her out from tossing a bear or a tiger down the hallway a hundred times, she'll set the stuffed animal down, crawl into my lap, and paw at my hand as if to say, *Pet me, pet me!* See? So cute!

Next on the list is my best friend, Isabel. What can I say about Isabel? She's the best friend a girl could have. She used to live in the duplex next to ours, but they moved last summer so her mom could open a cupcake shop. The shop is called It's Raining Cupcakes, and Isabel and her parents live in an apartment above it. I think it's pretty great, and I'm happy her mom is living out her dream, but I miss having Isabel right next door. We still see each other a lot, but won't this weekend, which brings me to the actual reason the world feels like a big, rotten tomato.

Isabel is out of town, in New York City, so she can't be a part of my cheer-myself-up plan. In fact, her being in New York City is the reason I'm not happy. She entered a baking contest through a magazine and her recipe was good enough to earn her a spot in the bake-off. The finalists all flew to New York this morning, where they'll compete in the bake-off tomorrow.

I'm the one who told Isabel about the contest. I'm glad she got to go, but I wanted to go too! I wanted to compete for the grand prize of one thousand dollars. That's a lot of money, and it would have paid for some singing and acting lessons, something I really want to do so I can be an actress someday.

When I woke up this morning, it hit me pretty hard that Isabel was in New York City while I was stuck here, in the small town of Willow, and my happiness quickly disappeared. It'll be back one of these days—hopefully by the time Isabel gets home and tells me whether or not she won the contest.

In the meantime, back to my list. Musicals. I love, love, LOVE musicals. Movies like *The Sound of Music*, *The Wizard of Oz*, *Annie*, *Hairspray*, *Mamma Mia!*, and *High School Musical*. I have a whole collection of musical movies I've gotten as gifts since I was six years old. When I'm feeling down, I pop one in and snuggle up with my favorite blanket and a good snack. Soon everything fades away. In fact, it fades away so much that halfway through the movie, I'm usually up and singing along. I can't help it! It's like I want to be in the movie singing those songs so bad, I just have to get up and do the closest thing to it—singing and dancing around in my bedroom (usually in my purple pajamas).

Fourth on the list is shopping. I don't even have to buy anything, it's just fun to look at all of the cool clothes, sparkly jewelry, and beautiful shoes. Sometimes I'll try on shoes I know my mom would never approve of in a million years and pretend I'm a movie star with a red-carpet event I have to attend. You know, like it's absolutely crucial that I have the right pair of shoes. Now that's a type of pretending I don't mind at all.

Finally, chocolate. There's a little plaque that hangs in our kitchen. It's been there for as long as I can remember. It says HAND OVER THE CHOCOLATE AND NO ONE GETS HURT. I can just imagine a bank robber going into a bank, strolling up to the counter, and saying those words. At first, the bank teller is terrified. But when the robber demands chocolate instead of money, the teller says, "Oh, honey, I sure do understand. It's been one of those days, huh?"

I love chocolate. It's definitely my snack of choice, when given an option. I know, I know. I should be eating apples, bananas, and carrots, and I do eat those things, I swear! But like my mom always says— everything in moderation.

Last summer, as I thought about a cupcake recipe for the *Baker's Best* baking contest, I knew I wanted my recipe to include chocolate. I mean, if you have two flavors of cupcakes sitting side by side, one with chocolate and one without, I bet people choose the chocolate one most of the time. The recipe I finally ended up submitting for my entry was one for watermelon chocolate cupcakes—chocolate cake with a watermelon-flavored frosting. (See? I like fruit, too!) My whole family thought they were amazing. But I guess the judges didn't agree. Stupid judges.

Stupid sadness and jealousy.

When I get home, I put my bike in the garage and go in the house. Daisy greets me at the door with her usual jumping, spinning, and *pet me, pet me* routine.

"Hello, adorable dog of mine and number one on my list," I whisper, petting her as she rolls over, giving me her belly to scratch.

After a sufficient amount of scratching time, I stand up. "Come on, Daisy. You want a treat?"

She follows me into the kitchen, her tail wagging so hard it's practically picking her up off the ground. I toss her a Milk-Bone, get a spoon from the silverware drawer, and then grab the chocolate ice cream from the freezer.

I don't even get a bowl. I sit on a stool at the counter and dig in.

"Sophie, is that you?" Mom calls from the other room.

"No, it's a stranger raiding your freezer."

Mom appears, smiling. I have to say, my mom is so cute. No, not Daisy-cute, but girlie-cute, I guess. She wears her blond hair short but stylish, and she has a round face with big blue eyes. And she always wears the cutest clothes, not like she's trying to be sixteen again, just fresh and fun. Today she's wearing jeans and a pink T-shirt that says WAG MORE, BARK LESS.

"Hi, honey. How was school today?"

I shrug my shoulders, partly because I don't want to tell her about my rotten tomato day and partly because my mouth is full of chocolatey, creamy goodness.

"I've been thinking about you," she says. "Thinking about how you're probably a little sad to be here and not in New York City like Isabel."

The way she looks at me and the way her caring comes through in her voice, I feel tears rising up. I blink hard a few times, then I shrug again, scared that if I try to talk about it, I'll have a full-blown tearfest going on. And I don't want that. The whole point of the chocolate ice cream is to cheer myself up!

"I have a surprise for you," she says, her face now literally beaming.

I swallow my mouthful of ice cream. Thoughts of a tearfest disappear at the mention of the word "surprise." I totally forgot that's another one on my list of pick-me-ups! Except, it's sort of hard to make a surprise happen by myself.

I wait, my spoon frozen in midair.

She brings her hand around from behind her back, and she's holding three tickets. I lean in, my eyes squinting, trying to read the small words.

My spoon makes a loud clanking noise as I drop it on to the counter and grab the tickets from her hand.

I can't believe it.

Wicked, the musical.

We're going to see *Wicked*!

Chapter 2

chocolate-covered peanuts

THEY SING AND DANCE IN YOUR MOUTH

I squeal, jump off my stool, and grab my mom so hard that I'm afraid for a second I might have broken her rib or something.

I let go. "Sorry, are you okay?"

She laughs. "Yes. Are you?"

"Mom, how did you get these? When—?"

"One of my customers has a sister with some

connections to Broadway Across America. Good ones, obviously. When I heard *Wicked* was coming to Portland, I asked if she could help me get some tickets. And so she did."

I can't believe it. Other kids at school have seen the show when they've traveled to places like New York City, San Francisco, and Miami, and they always come back raving about it. The story, the songs, the performances—all of it is supposed to be spectacular to watch. I've read it's the story of how the Wicked Witch of the West in *The Wizard of Oz* came to be wicked.

"When is it?" I ask.

"Tomorrow night."

"There are three tickets here," I say, grabbing the rapidly melting ice cream and sticking it back in the freezer. "Who else is going with us?"

"I thought you might want to ask a friend to come along. If not, Hayden might like to see it."

Ugh. Hayden. Okay, my eight-year-old brother is definitely not on my list of pick-me-ups. In fact, he just might have the ability to totally ruin what could turn out to be one of the best nights of my entire life.

My brain goes through my list of friends from

the theater camps I've attended the last few years. Choosing one of them makes sense because I know they would love a live musical production as much as I would.

"Lily!" I decide. "I'll ask Lily. She's perfect. I hope she can go."

"Better call her right away," Mom says. "If she's free, tell her we'll pick her up at four tomorrow. We'll stop and get a bite to eat on the way. The play starts at seven. We'll be home really late, so maybe ask if she can spend the night with us."

"Okay." I give my mom another hug, a much gentler one this time. "Thanks, Mom. You are now officially on my pick-me-up list."

She smiles. "That's a good thing, right?"

"You're on there with chocolate! Yes, it's a good thing."

As I'm heading to the phone, Hayden comes in carrying what looks to be a spaceship made out of toilet-paper tubes. He's obsessed with all things outer space.

"Hayden," Mom asks with a funny look on her face. "Where did you get those?"

"Mom, don't worry," he says. "I got them out without unrolling all the paper. Well, except for one. And I folded the paper up really neatly. Anyway, with most of them, you can hardly tell the tubes are gone!"

I grab the phone and take it to my room, and leave Mom alone to handle that situation.

Lily is really excited. Her parents give her permission to come with us and spend the night so I give her all the details. After I hang up, I lie on my bed, thinking of all the fun times we had together at theater camps and missing them.

Last summer, the only camp I went to was the two-week overnight camp my parents have sent me to the last few years. It wasn't nearly as fun as theater camp, although two good things did happen. One, I met this cute guy named Kyle who was really nice. Well, I thought he was nice. He never wrote to me or called me like he promised. Okay, scratch that. One good thing happened. One of the camp counselors, Marcella, recorded everyone's talent show performances. She said she was so impressed by my performance, she planned on showing it to her mom. I thought that was a strange thing to do until she explained that her mom is an agent, and she's always looking for talented young people to star in commercials and TV shows. Of course, here it is November, a long way from July, and Marcella hasn't gotten in touch with me.

That does it. Overnight camp was a complete bomb. Which is why I'm going to do everything possible so I don't have to go next year and can go back to theater camp here in Willow instead. I just need to figure out a way to make some money for lessons. Otherwise, I'm afraid they'll give me the role of a tree or something else equally humiliating. I'm so much more than a tree, I know I am!

When I leave my room to tell Mom that Lily is going with us to the play, I hear Hayden talking in the bathroom. "But, Mom, why is the tube so important? The toilet paper will still get the job done, right?"

On Saturday, Mom and I spend almost the whole day getting ready for our big evening. Mom gives us both manicures after we eat lunch, and then we go through all of our clothes before we settle on what dresses we're going to wear. I decide to wear a pale-green dress I wore to a wedding last year that still fits. Mom chooses a simple black dress she said she's had forever, because it's the kind of dress that never goes out of style.

After that, I curl my shoulder-length blond hair and put in two small, sparkly barrettes to dress it up a little. When we finally head out to the family room to say good-bye to Dad and Hayden, Dad whistles at us.

"Who are you and what have you done with my wife and daughter?"

We laugh and then Hayden says, "Eh, Sophie, you look better in your purple pajamas."

I give him a swat with the small handbag Mom lent me.

"Drive safely," Dad says as he kisses Mom on the cheek. "And enjoy the show." Then he leans in and kisses me on the forehead. His breath smells like peanuts.

"It's going to be so awesome," I say.

"Oh, wait a second!" Dad hustles into the kitchen and pulls out a bag of chocolate-covered peanuts. "Here, take these along. They'll have snacks during the intermission, but they'll cost almost as much as the tickets to the show."

Mom sticks them in her purse and then we say good-bye.

As I put my seat belt on, I turn and look at my beautiful mom. "I'm not dreaming, am I? We're really doing this?"

"I promise, you are wide-awake." And then she starts singing, "We're off to see the wizard . . ."

And I burst out laughing.

Chapter 3

chocolate-chip pancakes

TRY THEM FOR A SWEET SUNDAY

MORNING BREAKFAST

*T*he play is incredible.

Brilliant.

Dazzling!

I laugh. I cry. I cheer! We all do. When it's over and the actors take the stage for their bows, I applaud as hard as I can, wishing there was another performance so we could experience the magic all over again.

"I'm pretty sure that was the most amazing thing I've ever seen," Lily says as we stand in line waiting to buy a CD. We want to listen to it on the way home. I look at her and realize she's glowing, and it's not because of the sparkly coral dress she's wearing.

"Me too!" I say.

We get our CD and head outside. The night is cold and clear. I look up, but the tall buildings of downtown Portland prevent me from seeing the moon or very many stars. We rush to the parking garage, shivering the whole way. When we get in the car, Mom turns it on and cranks up the heat.

I lean in toward the front seat. "Just so you know, I'm now more determined than ever to find a way to pay for some singing and acting lessons."

"You need to help me come up with the hottest look in doggy fashion," she says as she puts the car in reverse. "We could make millions. Then you'd be set."

I turn and look at Lily, who has a puzzled look on her face. "My mom designs and sews clothes for dogs. Her company is called The Pampered Pooch."

"That's, um, different," she says, trying to be nice. Both Mom and I laugh.

"Do you have a dog, Lily?" Mom asks her.

"No. Just a big yellow cat."

"So you probably don't get the whole doggy-fashion thing."

"Not really," she says. "I mean, don't they already have fur coats?"

I reach over and tap Mom's shoulder. "See? Isn't that exactly what I said when you told me you were going to start the business?"

"Well, if you ever have a good idea for a new doggy look, Lily, be sure and let me know. Sophie's acting career may depend on it."

I pop open our new CD and hand it to Mom to put into the car's player. And just like that, we're back in the magical world of Galinda, Elphaba, and Fiyero once again.

The next morning, Lily and I make chocolate-chip pancakes. Hayden comes in, jumps up and down, and tells us that last night he finally convinced Dad to let him watch *Star Wars*. They have a movie date next Friday night, and lucky me, I'm invited too.

"I've waited my whole life to see *Star Wars*," he tells us. "I didn't think I could go on a minute longer. Out of all my friends, I'm the only one who hasn't seen any of the movies. But now it's finally going to happen."

For once, I can actually relate to my annoying little brother. "That's how I felt about *Wicked*. I'm happy for you, Little Brother Man. So why does Dad think you're suddenly ready?"

"I told him it wasn't fair that you got to see *Wicked* on stage. So I told him to give me one good reason why I couldn't finally see *Star Wars*."

"What'd he say?"

Hayden takes a big piece of pancake, dips it in the syrup, and shoves it in his mouth. "He couldn't think of anything, Soph. Not one reason! So he looked at me and said, 'Okay, Hayden. Next weekend. *Star Wars*, here we come.'"

He's done eating in about two minutes flat, thank goodness. "Catch you girls later. I've got a top-secret project I have to finish."

"Don't touch the toilet paper!" I yell.

"Funny kid," Lily says. "He reminds me of that one boy Henry, at theater camp. Do you remember him?"

"Oh, the supersmart kid who memorized every single president of the United States, including their dates of birth? Yeah, I remember."

We're quiet for a second, both of us lost in the memories.

"Lily, the last time we talked, you said you were thinking about taking voice lessons. Did you sign up?"

"Yeah, I did."

"Do you like them? I mean, are they fun?"

She shrugs and takes another bite of pancake. "I don't know if fun is the right word. My teacher really pushes me. But yeah, I like them."

Envy tugs at my heart. "You have such a beautiful voice," I tell her. "I bet you'll be on a stage someday, singing and acting."

She blushes, and tucks her straight brown hair behind her ear. "I don't know. I hope so. It's what I want more than anything."

"Yeah. Me too," I say as we put our dishes in the dishwasher. "So what do you want to do now?"

"I've been dying to see your friend's cupcake shop. Could we walk over there?" She checks the clock on the microwave. "My mom won't be here for another couple of hours."

Lily lives on the other side of Willow and is in eighth grade at the other middle school in town. I'm surprised she hasn't made a trip to the cupcake shop yet. When she mentions it, I think of Isabel and the baking contest. Maybe Isabel's grandma, who's running the shop while Isabel and her mom are out of town, will know who won the contest. I'd love to find out!

"Sure. Just let me tell my mom where we're going."

When we get outside, it feels cool and crisp. No rain, luckily. The walk goes quickly as we talk about school, the play, and theater camp.

"I'm so glad you called me," she says as we turn the corner, It's Raining Cupcakes now in sight. "I mean, not just because of the play. It's been fun, hanging out with you."

I smile. "Yeah, it's been really fun."

When we get up to the shop, a closed sign hangs from the door. We both mutter "oh no" at the sight.

Lily peeks in the window. "It's adorable! Wow, look at that gorgeous mural on the wall."

"Yeah, it's very cute," I say. "Sorry they're not open. Guess we'll have to come back another time."

"It's a date," she says.

Just as we turn to head back home, Stan, Isabel's neighbor, comes through the door that leads to the apartments above the shops. He owns the barbershop that sits next door to It's Raining Cupcakes. He's supernice.

"Sophie!" Stan says. "So wonderful to see you." He gives me a strange look. "You know Isabel doesn't get back until tomorrow, right? Or did you come by to get a haircut from your favorite barber?"

I laugh. "No. See, my friend Lily here wanted to see the shop and have a cupcake. I forgot they're not open on Sundays. Have you heard anything about Isabel?"

"Haven't heard a thing," he says. "And I'm dying to know too! You could go up and knock on their door. I bet her dad is home and he probably has the answer."

I wave my hand. "No, that's okay. I'll wait and hear

it from Isabel. I'm sure she wants to be the one to tell me anyway."

He looks at Lily. "Well, I hope you do come back. From what I hear, they could really use the business."

I get a funny feeling in my stomach when he says that. "What? What do you mean? Are things not going well?"

His round cheeks turn a rosy-pink. "Oh for Pete's sake, look at me, spouting off things that are none of my business. I do apologize."

"No, it's fine. I mean, I won't say anything to Isabel about it. Are things really bad? What have you heard?"

He looks down at the ground for a second, then back at me. "Let's just say, in the words of Isabel's grandma, things are far from ducky in the cupcake world."

"That's awful," I say softly. "Isabel hasn't said anything to me about it. I wonder if she knows?"

"I sure know how to ruin the mood, don't I?" Stan says. "I better turn it around quickly! Knock, knock."

Lily gives me a funny look.

I shrug. "He loves 'em."

"Who's there?" she asks.

"Icy," Stan says.

"Icy who?"

"Icy you again someday soon, okay?"

We wave and start walking home. My feet feel heavy, like my shoes are bricks. I don't want to go home. I want to do something to help Isabel's family. But what? There's not one thing I'd be able to do.

"You okay?" Lily asks.

"I just feel bad for Isabel and her family. They've worked so hard. I don't want their business to fail, you know?"

"I bet Beatrice's Brownies has made it hard on them," Lily says. "Their location is better. And their brownies are so good. We've probably been there ten times since it's opened."

My heart sinks even more. I bet Lily's family is like a lot of families. Beatrice's Brownies is a big chain, with stores all across the country. They put a lot of money into advertising, something a small business like It's Raining Cupcakes can't do.

Lily must sense it's time to change the subject.

"So what's going on with Isabel? I didn't quite get what you guys were talking about."

"She's in New York," I explain. "She competed in this big baking contest yesterday. If she wins, she brings home a check for a thousand dollars."

She smiles. "That'd be awesome. Do you think her parents will let her keep it all? And what would she do with money like that?"

"Isabel wants to travel. We dream of being onstage while Isabel dreams of seeing beautiful places."

"Wish I'd known about that contest," Lily says.

"No, because then you'd probably be in New York City too, and you would have missed going to see *Wicked* with me."

"You're totally right. That performance was worth way more than a thousand dollars anyway."

Yeah. I like how this girl thinks.

Chapter 4

chocolate milk

IT COMES FROM SWEET COWS

Before Isabel left, we agreed to meet at the
Blue Moon Diner right after she got home so she
could tell me if she'd been crowned Queen of the
Baking Contest.

At school on Monday, it seems like National Ask-
About-Isabel Day. Everywhere I go, someone asks
me if I've heard from her yet. I try to keep my face
happy and my answer short—"Nope, not yet, but I'm

seeing her after school." By the end of the day, I'm exhausted. I head home, and even there, I'm not safe from interrogation.

I walk through the door and give Daisy a good belly rub. Hayden comes up to me and asks, "Sophie, when does Isabel get back?"

"She should be back by now. We're meeting up in an hour."

"I've heard aliens love New York City. What if she didn't make it home? What if they abducted her and instead of making it back home to Oregon, she's somewhere in outer space, trying to send us a message so we can save her?"

I shake my head. I've given up trying to tell my brother there is no such thing as aliens. "Hayden, that's a good point. I think you better try to construct a device to receive the message they're trying to send."

His eyes got as big as flying saucers. "Really? What do you think the device should be made out of?"

I think on this for a few seconds. "Tape. Lots and lots of really sticky tape. And paper, of course. The expensive kind Dad keeps in his top desk drawer. Good luck, Little Brother Man."

Before he turns to go, he gives me a big grin and a full-on salute. Finally, a little respect. I'll have to give orders involving aliens more often.

I sit down at the kitchen table, pull a textbook out of my backpack, and try to read. But my brain just can't focus. So then I go to the bathroom to freshen up, which means putting on some bubblegum lip gloss and running a brush through my hair. Thirty seconds later, I check my watch. Fifty more excruciating minutes. I'm about to go to my bed and lie down because death by waiting seems inevitable at this point, when the phone rings.

I hear Mom answer it as I come out of the bathroom. Then she calls, "Sophie, where are you? It's for you."

It has to be Isabel. Maybe her plane's delayed. Or maybe she's extremely excited, and she can't wait to tell me. Or, maybe she's feeling too high-and-mighty to meet up with a low-life peasant like me, and wants to cancel our plans.

"Who is it?" I whisper.

"A girl named Marcella?"

My counselor from summer camp. How weird that I was just thinking about her the other day.

"Hello?"

"Sophie! It's Mar! How are you?"

"I'm fine. How are you?"

"Fantastic! Listen, I have great news. I finally got around to showing my mom your talent show performance this past weekend when I was home from college. She thinks you are just the cutest thing."

"She does?"

"Yes! Of course she does. I told you, that performance was totally impressive. Anyway, my mom is hoping you and your mom might be willing to call and talk to her about signing with her talent agency in Los Angeles. She thinks she could get you into some commercials really easily. Maybe even a spot on a TV show. You have the looks, you have the voice—actually, you've got it all, according to her."

I look at my mom, then back at the phone. Is this for real? Commercials? TV shows?

"Sophie?" Marcella asks.

"Sorry. I—I think I'm in shock. Are you serious?"

She laughs. "Would I joke about something like this? Get a piece of paper so I can give you her phone number. She's really excited to talk with you."

Somehow I manage to make it over to the counter where I find a pen and notepad. After she gives me the number, I thank her and we hang up.

"What was that about?" Mom asks.

I speak slowly, as if I need to hear it coming out of my mouth to believe it. "One of my camp counselors says her mom wants me to sign with her agency."

"Agency? What kind of agency?"

I look at the phone. I look at my mom. It *really* happened. I grab Mom's hands and start jumping up and down. I can't even talk for a few seconds. Finally I yell, "Mom, a talent agency! Like, for actors. She saw a recording of my talent show performance, and she thinks I've got it all! Those were her exact words!"

Mom pulls me to her and wraps her arms around me. "Oh, Sophie, that's wonderful. Should we call her now?"

The clock on the microwave tells me if I don't leave soon, I might be late for my diner date with Is. But a talent agent wants to talk to me!

I go to the fridge and chug some chocolate milk right out of the container. When I'm done, I wipe the milk mustache away and I smile. "Yeah. Let's call her!"

Chapter 5

french fries dipped in a chocolate shake

A GREAT SWEET-AND-SALTY SNACK

When I finally get to the Blue Moon, Isabel is in a booth, waiting for me. Her face, along with the empty water glass sitting in front of her, tells me she's been here for a while.

"Chickarita," I say as I slide into the seat across from her. "Sorry I didn't get here sooner. Something of epic proportions came up and I couldn't get away."

"I was beginning to wonder if you'd forgotten about me," she says as she picks at a hangnail.

The waitress walks up to our table, and we order our usual: chocolate shakes and French fries.

After she leaves, I lean in and wait until Isabel's brown eyes meet mine. "I'm sorry. I'm here now, right? So tell me! Tell me everything! Did you win?"

A smile spreads across her face like the sun breaking through the clouds, and in that moment, I know. I know she came here, flying on her bike, ready to tell me she won and then she waited and waited some more. Her enthusiasm must have deflated like a balloon with a leak in it.

"I won," she says. Then, like she almost can't believe it, she says it again, louder. "Sophie, I really won!"

I clap my hands together and squeal. A few people look over at me, which makes us both laugh. "Oh. My. Gosh. Isabel! This is the coolest thing EVER! Tell me. Tell me what happened!"

"The day of the bake-off, I was so nervous. I mean, it's one thing baking in your own kitchen, but it's another thing to bake in this big convention center where they have a bunch of little kitchens set up, one for each contestant. And the whole time I was in my little kitchen, I kept thinking, judges *are going to be eating what I make*. It was pretty scary."

"Wow," I say. "So you got there and they had all the ingredients for your cupcakes, and you just started baking?"

She smiles. "Yes. Except I didn't make cupcakes. I made chocolate jam tarts. Mom sent in the recipe I'd wanted to do all along. She felt bad, I guess, about wanting me to submit a cupcake recipe. Anyway, the chocolate jam tart recipe is the recipe they wanted me to make. And luckily, the day of the bake-off, everything went really well, and the tarts turned out perfectly. Some of the other contestants had a terrible time with their recipes, burning things or forgetting to add important ingredients. I'm pretty sure, on a different day, mine wouldn't have won. I feel so lucky!"

"You are talented, Is, not lucky. And can I just say that chocolate jam tarts sound so delicious. And different! Will you make them for me sometime?"

"I think Mom is going to feature them at the cupcake shop next month. You can come every day in December and have one if you want."

The waitress brings our order and we dig in as Is tells me about New York City and all the things they did while they were there. They visited a fancy cupcake shop, climbed to the top of the Empire State Building, and saw a Broadway musical.

"Which one?" I ask.

"*Wicked!*"

"No way! Are you serious? I saw *Wicked* this weekend too, in Portland. My mom got tickets and surprised me. Wasn't it good?"

"I loved it," she says. "I kept thinking, someday Sophie will be in a play like this."

I smile. Isabel pauses to take a sip of her shake, then she says, "I wish you could have been there, Sophie Bird. We would have had so much fun."

"It's all right, Chickarita. I'm over it. Sort of." I take a napkin and dab at my eyes. It makes her laugh.

"So, what are you going to do with the prize money?" I ask. And when I do, I realize any jealousy I felt is gone. I'm truly happy for her. She totally deserves it.

Her face lights up. "Oh! It's going to be so fun. My parents and I are going to spend a few days up in Seattle. See, at the bake-off, there was a boy in the kitchen next to me named Jack. When I asked him what he was baking, he said, 'I can't tell you, because I'm on a secret baking mission. If I told you, I'd have to kill you.' And I said, 'Wow, you mean they really let spies into this thing?' And then he leaned over and whispered, 'No, actually, they don't. And you better not breathe a word of our conversation to anyone, understand?' Anyway, Jack lives in Seattle and his mom owns Penny's Pie Place. Doesn't it sound cute? My mom wants to see it! And since I've never been to Seattle—"

"Isabel, wait a second." I raise my eyebrows. "Do you *like* Jack?"

She gives me this shrug that says, *I'm not going to admit it, but I'm pretty sure I do.* "I don't know. All I know is that he's nice and really funny."

I smile. "I think I know how you feel."

She starts to say something, but I wave my hand and say, "No! We aren't going to talk about the rotten-boy-from-camp-whose-name-must-never-be-spoken-again. So just forget about it. It's over and that's that. When are you going to Seattle?"

"During winter break, in December. We'll get to see the city all decorated in lights! And, Sophie, here's the best part: Mom and Dad said I could invite you to go with us!"

"Really? Me and you in Seattle?"

"I know, right? So you have to ask your parents when you get home, okay?"

"Okay, I will."

"Can I get you girls anything else?" the waitress asks. We tell her no thanks and go to work finishing off the fries.

"Oh, before I forget, I brought you something," Isabel says.

She reaches into the pocket of her jacket and pulls out a little notebook. It has a picture of the New York skyline across the front with the words I ♥ NEW YORK.

I smile. "Thanks, Is. It's cute! Not sure what I'll write in it, but I'll think of something."

"Yeah, you'll think of something," she says. "Hey, hold on. What thing of epic proportions happened before you got here? You haven't said."

The butterflies I felt earlier as I talked on the phone with Mrs. Parks come rushing back. I still can't believe how my whole life has changed in the course of an hour.

"Well, it turns out one of my camp counselors, Marcella, has a mom who is a talent agent. And she's interested in signing me. She thinks she can get me into some commercials, and maybe even a spot on a TV show."

Isabel's brown eyes get big and round, like two chocolate cupcakes. "Sophie! Why didn't you say anything sooner? That's ten times more exciting than me winning a baking contest. You're going to be famous!"

I laugh. "Well, it's kind of early to be saying that. She's sending me a contract and we have to mail her some photos, then she'll let me know if there are any auditions that might be a good fit. I'm trying not to get my hopes up, you know?"

Ah, who am I kidding? My hopes are already higher than Seattle's Space Needle!

Chapter 6

chocolate gum

IT WILL SATISFY THAT CHOCOLATE
CRAVING IN A PINCH

Tuesday morning, I roll out of bed, take a shower, and get ready. When I get to the kitchen for breakfast, Dad hands me the *Willow Gazette*. I squeal when I see my best friend's picture with the heading "Isabel Browning Takes First Place in National Baking Contest." I read the entire article and when I'm finished, I'm so excited. Today will be a really fun day for Isabel.

"It's exciting!" Dad says. "She won a thousand bucks? Somehow you left out that small detail when you were telling us about it last night. Guess you were too busy thinking about the talent agent who wants to sign you, huh?"

I smile. "Yeah. That could be it. Oh, and Isabel wants to spend the money on a trip to Seattle with her family. She asked me to come too. Can I go? It'll be over winter break."

"I don't see why not. Sounds fun. Check with Mom, though. Make sure she isn't secretly planning a family trip to Tahiti or something."

"Wow, that'd be some surprise. Even better than tickets to see *Wicked*."

I scarf down a piece of toast and some juice, and then I'm out the door and on my way to school. What a difference a few days make. There will be no fake happiness today. Only the real kind, thank goodness.

When I get to school, a crowd has gathered around Isabel. I try to squeeze my way in, but I don't have much luck. I can hear some kids laughing, and then Isabel says something so quietly, I can't make it out.

When the first warning bell rings, everyone takes off, and I'm able to get to our locker, where Isabel is standing.

"Congratulations!" I say, reaching in to get my science textbook. "You made the front page of the paper! And they mentioned the cupcake shop. I bet that will help business."

She looks at me funny. "Why would you say that?"

Uh-oh. "I mean, it's a good thing, that's all. Good for you, good for your parents. It was a great article!"

I slam our locker and look at her. "You okay? You don't seem as happy as I thought you'd be."

"You know how the paper mentioned the prize money?" she whispers.

I nod. "Yeah. So?"

"A couple of the kids were joking about it just now. One said I'd probably be going on a shopping spree and would come back with a new Coach purse or something. Then the other one said after that I'd be too good to eat in the cafeteria with them, and I'd have to eat with the teachers instead."

I feel my happiness disappearing faster than a

plate of jam tarts at a coffee shop. "Isabel, don't let them bug you. They're just jealous, that's all."

She bites her lip, quiet for a second. Then she says, "I told them I was taking my family on a trip. Someone said they'd watch for me on the *Spoiled Rich Kids* TV show."

Anger boils up inside of me. "Isabel, listen. You have nothing to feel bad about! You came up with an incredible recipe, and you worked hard to bake that recipe in a bake-off with real judges! Don't let their stupid jealousy bring you down." The words taste yucky in my mouth, because I know, just a few days ago, I was one of those stupid, jealous people. Shame on me. Shame on them.

We start walking to class. "They're acting like I won a million dollars or something," she says.

"Now *that* would be something, huh? You could buy every girl in the whole school a Coach purse."

As I'm turning into my science class, Dennis Holt, a tall, skinny kid I've known since kindergarten, is there and says, "You're buying every girl in the whole school a purse, Isabel? Wow, you *are* rich. What about the boys? What do we get? Maybe a new video game? There's this new one I really want—"

I interrupt him. "She's not buying anyone anything. Especially you." I wave to Isabel. "See you next period."

The bell rings just as I'm taking my seat. Mr. Leonard tells us we'll be doing an experiment with chewing gum. He loves coming up with these crazy experiments to help us learn what all the terms in the scientific method mean. This time, we'll be chewing different kinds of bubblegum to see which type of gum blows the biggest bubble.

I like Mr. Leonard except for the fact that he doesn't let us choose our partners. He seems to get a thrill out of matching me with kids who get on my nerves. For the bubblegum experiment, of course, he assigns Dennis Holt as my partner, who is definitely on my nerves today.

"Hey, Sophie, want to see a dead bird's foot?" Dennis asks when he comes to my desk to work.

Ewww! "What? Why would I want to see that? And why do you have a dead bird's foot? That's disgusting."

He's rummaging around in his binder, like he's looking for it. If he shows it to me, things are going to get ugly. "My cat likes to kill things and bring them to the porch for us to see. The bird's foot was lying there, so I picked it up."

I hold up my hands. "Please, do not show me that thing. And what do you mean, foot? Birds don't have feet, do they?"

"Yes, they do."

I scowl. "No. I'm pretty sure they don't."

"What are they called, then?" he asks.

"Talons. At least on big birds of prey that's what they're called. My brother went through a birds of prey obsession."

"Man, I bet he'd like to see the bird's foot," Dennis mumbles.

I shake my head. Why do boys have to be so weird most of the time? "Can we just get started with the project? Please?"

"Sure." He points to the pieces of gum in front of us. "Pick a flavor, any flavor."

I don't say one word to him the whole time, even though he tries his hardest to get me to talk to him. I simply shake my head yes or no if I have to answer an important question. Halfway through class, I can tell he's getting tired of my silent act.

Mr. Leonard comes over to see how we're doing. He gives us his approval, then says, "You both need to work on the write-up. Don't forget, it's due on Friday. Sophie, I do not want you doing all of the work, understand?"

I look at Dennis, expecting him to make a smart remark, but he just sits there, twirling a gum wrapper between his fingers.

"Okay," I say.

After he leaves, Dennis says, "He hates me."

"He does not hate you. He might think you're lazy, but he doesn't hate you."

"Do you think I'm lazy?" he asks.

I unwrap another piece of gum and pop it in my mouth. Oh my gosh, it tastes like chocolate. Chocolate gum!?

"That depends," I tell him. "How much of the write-up are you going to do? And you have to taste this chocolate gum. It's the weirdest thing."

"Do you want me to do all of it? I can do the entire

write-up if you want me to. I'll prove to both of you I'm not lazy."

I don't trust him with the whole thing. "How about half? You want to do the first half or the second half?"

"I have a better idea," he says. "Let's meet up one day after school and do the whole thing together. How about Thursday? I have other stuff going on after school tomorrow."

I'm silent.

"I promise it'll be fun. And my mom makes really good snacks."

"There's one more thing you have to promise," I tell him. "That after class, you'll go and tell Isabel congratulations on the contest. Tell her you're really happy for her, and mean it. Plus, I want you to apologize for joking about the money."

He sighs. "Fine. But I really don't think what I said was that big of a deal."

"Imagine twenty other kids saying something like it," I tell him. "It *is* a big deal."

His expression changes. I can tell he gets it.

"All right. Sorry."

"Don't tell me. Tell her."

He nods. "Where do you want to meet Thursday?"

I consider the question for a second. "My brother says Mars is pretty cool."

"Ha ha, very funny. How about my house?"

So much for a day filled with real happiness.

Chapter 7

chocolate-covered banana

DIP IT IN PEANUT BUTTER

FOR AN EXTRA KICK

By the time the bell rings, I get the feeling Isabel would love nothing more than to return to New York City and stay there forever.

"Want to come over?" I ask her as we leave school. The sun is shining, but it's cold. I zip my black down jacket all the way up. "We can listen to the *Wicked* CD. Bake some cookies or something?"

She slips her arms through her backpack straps as we walk toward the bike rack. "Thanks, Soph, but I better get home. I have lots of homework. I missed two days of school, remember?"

A strange noise comes from above. We look up and see a flock of geese flying across the bright blue sky. A couple of them are honking loudly.

"Flying south for the winter," I say.

"Wish I could go with them," Isabel says.

"Oh, Isabel. The stupid, jealous people need to get over it and just be happy for you." Yes, once again I think of myself when I say this, and secretly cringe. "Try to forget about them, okay?"

She bends down to unlock her bike. "I'm trying, but it's hard. I heard someone whispering to a friend that I think I'm better than everyone else now. Where did she get that?"

She stands up and looks at me, her eyes starting to fill with tears. "You've done nothing wrong," I tell her. "Nothing! So forget about them and just hang in there. It'll be old news in a couple of days anyway. Hey, you want me to do something shocking and get caught, so the attention is on me? Toilet paper the principal's house or something?"

She finally smiles. "Thanks for the thought, but no, please don't."

"Okay, well, if there's anything I can do, let me know."

"Sophie Bird, you are the best."

She gives me a quick hug before she gets on her bike and rides away. I look up and think of those geese, flying together in the V formation. They'll stick together and help each other through until they get to their final destination.

Why can't the kids at school be more like those geese?

I pull out the notebook she gave me and decide then and there it'll be a place where I can dream things, big or little, and maybe, just maybe, they'll come true.

Dream #1—
I dream of a school where
no one is mean to one another.
(In other words, everyone
is as sweet as cupcakes,
like my best friend.)

❀ ❀ ❀

When I get home, I find Mom at her sewing machine, working away on something for her Pampered Pooch business. Last year the business really took off and she got so busy, she had to hire a couple of women to help her. Now they also sew doggy clothes in their homes.

It's weird to me how many people believe dogs need clothes. When my mom first started Pampered Pooch a few years ago, Dad and I thought she'd be out of business in six months. Boy were we wrong. Not only do people want their dogs to have clothes, but they want them to have a variety. I mean, do they really think the neighbors are going to say bad things if the dog goes outside wearing the same outfit two days in a row? I guess they do. And thanks to my mom, there are some dogs out there who dress better than I do.

"What are you making?" I ask as I grab a banana from the fruit basket. Daisy begs me with her eyes, telling me she wants a little snack, too. So I take a treat from the special treat container and toss it to her.

"I'm working on bows today," she says.

I pick up a finished one. It's made out of plaid

fabric in pastel colors. In the center of the bow is a button shaped like a bone.

"You want one?" she asks. "I bet it'd look cute on you."

I smile. "Uh, no thanks. I'm good. Hey, what about that leather jacket idea I had? I bet it'd be a big seller."

She takes her scissors and cuts the thread. "I'm still thinking on that. Leather is expensive, so I think it's going to have to be a faux leather of some kind. And besides, dogs like to chew on leather. Can you imagine paying fifty dollars for a jacket and having your dog decide it makes a great chew toy?"

I open a jar of peanut butter and scoop some up with my banana. "I can't imagine paying fifty dollars for anything relating to my dog. I love her, but Mom, that's so ridiculous. Don't people realize there are starving children in Africa? I just think there are a lot more important things to spend money on."

She stands up. "Careful, honey. You're starting to make me feel bad. Although, if they weren't buying the stuff from me, they'd probably buy it somewhere else."

"Mom, I'm hungry," Hayden says as he walks into the kitchen.

I break off part of my banana and hand it to him. "Don't say I never gave you anything."

He takes a bite. "How come I taste peanut butter?"

"Because bananas and peanut butter are awesome together." I give him the peanut butter jar. "Here, try it."

"I'd rather dip it in chocolate. Do we have any of that?"

"Mom, is that okay?" I ask.

"Sure, go ahead."

I take the chocolate-flavored syrup out of the fridge and pour some in a bowl. I cut up Hayden's banana, put it on a plate, and set it all at the kitchen table.

"There you go. Dude, that's some snack you got there. You could even dip the banana slice in peanut butter *and* chocolate. Then you'd have it all."

He pulls a banana slice out of the bowl of chocolate with his fingers, and I watch as chocolate drips down his arm and all over his pants.

Mom glares at me as she grabs a towel and starts

cleaning up his gooey mess. "How about giving the kid a fork, Sophie? And maybe not quite so much chocolate next time?"

As I head to the silverware drawer, I notice Mom has gathered photos of me and piled them next to the phone. "Mom, you're not going to send all of these to Mrs. Parks, are you?"

"No, honey. I pulled them out so you could go through them and choose the ones you like the best."

"So does this mean you and Dad have discussed it?"

"Yes, we have. If this is something you really want to do, we'll support you. I've done some research and talked to some other clients, and Candace Parks is one of the top agents in the business."

"Are you going to be famous, Sophie?" Hayden asks before he licks the chocolate between his fingers on the hand Mom hasn't washed yet.

"Ha, that's what Isabel said. It's fun to imagine big things happening, I guess."

Mom goes to the sink to rinse out the chocolatey dish rag. "How is Isabel, anyway?" she asks. "Was everyone happy for her today at school?"

"Not really. Jealous is more like it. Everyone was focused on the prize money and acting like she's rich now or something. Wouldn't that be nice? Then their business wouldn't be in trouble."

Mom frowns. "Oh no. Sorry to hear that. And what's this about their business being in trouble? Did Isabel tell you that?"

"No, their neighbor, Stan. He let it slip when Lily and I walked over there the other day. Isabel hasn't said a word, and I don't know what to say."

"I'm thinking if she wants to talk about it with you, she'll bring it up. Maybe just wait and see."

I grab the jar of peanut butter and a sleeve of crackers and head for my room. "Okay. Thanks, Mom."

Once I'm in my room, I pull out the notebook Isabel gave me and write down two more dreams.

Dream #2—
I dream that someday
there are no hungry
children in Africa,
or anywhere else.

Dream #3—
I dream that tomorrow
Isabel is back to her
happy self again.

Chapter 8

candy cane dipped
in hot cocoa

A CHOCO-MINTY TREAT

There doesn't seem to be as much drama at school today. This is good. Still, Isabel seems quieter than usual, so I ask her to come over after school, using our upcoming social studies test on ancient Rome as a good reason. Studying together is much more fun than studying alone, I tell her. Mostly I just want to try and cheer her up! She agrees, so we ride our bikes to my house, then she calls her mom to let her know.

My mom made pumpkin bread, which we slice up and take to my room, along with two mugs of steaming hot cocoa.

"This bread is so good," I say. I hand her the plate. "Try some!"

Isabel takes a piece. "I love this time of year. Can you believe Thanksgiving is already next week?"

"I know—so many fun things to look forward to. And everyone bakes the yummiest things. I can't wait until Mom and I have our annual Christmas cookie baking day. Is your mom doing anything special with the cupcake shop for the holidays? Besides featuring your fabulous chocolate jam tarts?"

"So far, gingerbread cupcakes and peppermint cupcakes are on the menu, to get everyone in the holiday mood. She's really hoping we'll do a lot of business next month." She pauses. "I haven't said anything to you, but things aren't going very well. She's not even making enough money to pay the loan bill every month."

"Oh, Is, I'm sorry. But hopefully things will pick

up next month. So many people have holiday parties, you know?"

While she takes a sip of cocoa, her eyes light up. "Hey, I totally forgot to ask you about Seattle. Can you go?"

"Yes. Just let me know the dates, and I'll get it on our calendar."

"Okay, I have to check with Mom and Dad and see what they've decided."

We hear the phone ring, and a minute later, Mom pokes her head in. "Sophie, it's for you. It's Mrs. Parks. Do you want to call her back?"

Isabel looks at me. "Who's Mrs. Parks?"

"My agent," I say, smiling. "It's so weird saying that."

"Take it!" Isabel says, pointing toward the door. "Go on, you can't keep your agent waiting. Don't worry about me. I have Julius Caesar to keep me company."

"Okay, I'll be right back."

I step into the hallway and Mom hands me the phone. I shut Hayden's door as I walk by, so I won't be interrupted by Mr. Alien Hunter.

"Hi, Mrs. Parks," I say as I walk into the kitchen. I sit at the kitchen table, and Mom sits across from me.

"Please, Isabel, call me Candace. Mrs. Parks makes me feel old."

"Okay. Candace."

"Tell your parents thanks for overnighting the contract along with the photos. I'm going to ask your mom to take you to a professional photographer for some headshots, but for now, these will do. And I have good news."

I look at Mom and mouth the words "Good news!"

Candace continues. "An ad agency in Portland has put out a call for commercial auditions. It's a big client, and I think it'd be an excellent opportunity for you. The audition is the Monday after the Thanksgiving holiday. Are you interested?"

"Absolutely," I say.

"Wonderful. I'm going to drop all of the details about the audition in the mail to you. Please confirm with me once you receive it, all right?"

"Great, thanks, Mrs.—I mean Candace. Oh, wait, do you know what the commercial is for? I mean, what product I'd be selling?"

Mom gives me a thumbs-up. I think it means this is a good question to ask. "Of course," Candace says. "Sorry, I didn't mention that, did I? It's a wonderful company. I believe there's even a store there in your little town of Willow. Beatrice's Brownies?"

Oh no. I swallow hard. It couldn't be, could it? "Uh, what did you say?"

"Beatrice's Brownies. You've been there before, haven't you? Or are you the one person in a million who doesn't like brownies?"

"Yeah, I've been there," I say quietly.

"Wonderful! All right, Sophie, I have to run, but we'll talk again soon."

"Okay, bye."

"Sophie," Mom asks. "What is it? You look disappointed or something. Who's the commercial for?"

I want to cry. Why, out of the thousands of companies in America, does it have to be *that* one? Isabel's mom almost didn't open her cupcake shop because of Beatrice's Brownies. And now it may be one of the reasons It's Raining Cupcakes isn't doing very well.

Before I can say anything to Mom, Isabel appears. "Hey, Sophie, what'd your *agent* have to say? Don't you just love saying that? Your *agent*? Wait, let me guess. They want to give you your own TV show, right? A series?"

I force a laugh. "Yeah, right. She's working on a big deal for me. Huge! I can't even tell you guys, that's how big it is. She wants me to keep it to myself for now. Besides, I might jinx myself, you know?" I get up and pull on Isabel's arm. "Come on. Let's go study."

"But that's so silly," Isabel jokes. "You're going to be famous! You don't really need an education, do you?"

Oh, I need an education, all right. I need an education on how to choose between the opportunity of a lifetime and ruining my best friend's life.

Chapter 9

chocolate
mole sauce

TRY A HINT OF CHOCOLATE ON
YOUR NEXT ENCHILADA

Mom makes my favorite meal for dinner to celebrate the audition. The *Wicked* music plays softly in the background, "for ambiance," Mom says. She's trying to make it really special. All the music seems to be doing though is reminding me how much I want to be an actress, when I really want to forget that right now.

I haven't told her yet which company the audition is with. I said I'd wait and tell everyone at dinner. So now as we sit at the table in chicken enchilada heaven, I decide to break the horrible news. I can only hope my parents will forbid me from doing something that terrible to my best friend. Then all I have to do is call Candace back, cancel the audition, and sit back and wait for something else to come along. Please, oh please, let something else come along.

"Delicious, as always," my dad says, pausing after intense shoveling from plate to mouth to take a drink of water.

"Yeah, Mom," I say. "It's really good."

"Soph, tell Dad and Hayden your good news."

My dad turns and gives me the pirate look. I know, that sounds strange, but it's, like, this grin with one eye practically shut and he just looks like a pirate to me. Or he did when I was five, and the idea stuck. He's got the wavy brown hair, the beard, and the tanned, rugged face. My dad is an electrician, so he's nothing like some of my friends' dads who wear a suit to work everyday. Maybe if he was, I wouldn't be able to spot the hidden pirate in him.

I swallow the bite in my mouth, then take a sip of milk. "Well, I got a call today for a commercial audition."

Hayden does a fist pump. "You *are* going to be famous. I knew it!"

"Sophie, that's amazing," Dad says. He takes his napkin and wipes all around his beard and mustache. "So, what's the commercial for? An interesting product, I hope."

"Yeah, not bran cereal or something yucky like that," Hayden says.

"Oh, it's interesting all right," I say. I take a deep breath. "It's Beatrice's Brownies."

For a second, everyone's quiet. Then Mom blinks a couple of times and says, "Sophie, that's wonderful. That's right up your alley—you love desserts."

I set my fork down. "Mom, it's not wonderful. It's terrible."

"Why?" Dad asks. "I think it sounds fantastic."

Who are these people and what have they done with my family?

"Won't that make Isabel mad?" Hayden asks.

"Yes," I say, nodding. "Yes, Hayden, thank you. It's going to make Isabel very mad. Which is exactly why I can't do it."

Dad scoots his chair away from the table and leans back. "Sophie, this is about you and your dreams, not Isabel. She's a good friend. I think she'll understand."

I look back and forth between Mom and Dad. Mom. Then Dad. "No! You guys need to tell me I can't do it!"

Mom laughs. "Sophie, why would we do that? Don't you want to do it?"

"That's not the point. The point is that I—"

And then I stop. Because suddenly, I'm not sure what the point of arguing with them is exactly.

"Look, honey," Dad says, "if you want to do the commercial, do the commercial. It's not like you're doing it to spite your best friend. You're doing it because it's a good opportunity. And no one would want to deny their best friend a good opportunity. If it was the other way around, I'm sure you'd encourage her to go for it. Right?"

I stand up. "I don't know. I guess I thought you guys would see it the way I see it."

Mom stands up and gives me a quick hug. "Sweetheart, I see where you're coming from. But this is the kind of thing that could lead to bigger things—things that could help make your dream come true. At the very least, go to the audition and see what it's like."

"I agree," Dad says. "If nothing else, it's good practice for the next time."

"Sophie," Hayden says, "maybe they'd let you hold a cupcake in one hand and a brownie in the other."

If only it were that easy.

"Do you want any dessert?" Mom asks.

"I do!" Hayden says.

"No, thanks," I tell her. "Dessert is the last thing I want right now."

I go to my room.

Dream #4—
I dream of the ability
to do the right thing,
even when it's hard.

The next day, I do my best to avoid Isabel. I hang out in the library before school and go straight to science first period without going to the locker first.

Dennis catches me in the hallway outside of the classroom. "They're called feet," he tells me. "Not talons. At least on regular birds. You were wrong."

"Whatever," I mumble.

"Hey, I apologized to Isabel like I promised. I really am sorry. I didn't mean to upset her. Or you. So, we're good now, right?"

I look over at him. He seems to mean it.

"Anyway," he continues, pushing his glasses up with his finger, "I thought you might want to know birds do have feet. Not that I wanted to prove you wrong or anything. I was just, you know, curious."

"It's fine. I'm probably wrong about a lot of things."

And as soon as the words are out, I stop in my tracks.

"What?" he asks. "What is it?"

I shake my head. "Nothing." I look at Dennis. "Okay, have you ever thought you were absolutely, positively right about something? But then everyone else tells you maybe you aren't right after all, and you start to second-guess yourself, even though you *know* you're right?"

He gives me a blank stare. "No. Not really. Hey, do you think birds have ears?"

I laugh. I can't help it. It's so ridiculous, and I can't believe I'm spilling my guts, in a roundabout sort of way, to Dennis Holt.

"I have no idea," I tell him.

"Maybe we can research it," he says. "We're still doing homework at my house later, right?"

Oh no. With all of the stuff going on about the audition, I totally forgot. Well, at least if I see Isabel after school, I have a reason to rush off. "Yeah. I rode my bike. You don't live very far from here, right?"

"You remember! My birthday party in first grade was pretty awesome, huh?"

I shake my head. "You had a Power Rangers cake, Dennis. That was not awesome. At least, not to all the girls you invited."

He laughs. "Power Rangers, activate!"

The warning bell rings, so we start walking toward our classroom.

"I'll meet you at the bike rack after school," he says.

"Okay. And hey, Dennis?"

"Yeah?"

"You're not going to try and show me the dead bird's foot at your house, are you?"

"Don't worry. I know it's not everyone's thing. But, Sophie, I'm curious. What is your thing?"

And before I have time to think twice, the word comes out. "Acting." I let out a big sigh, because the truth really does sort of hurt. "My thing, right now, is acting."

"Cool," he says. "I bet you're good at it."

And all I can think is, *We'll see, Dennis. We'll see.*

Chapter 10

milk and chocolate-chip cookies

THEY MAKE HOMEWORK BEARABLE

When we walk into Dennis's house, it smells delicious, like we've just walked into a bakery.

"Hello!" a woman's voice calls out. "Dennis, I'm in the kitchen."

"Yeah, Mom, I can tell. Whatever you're making, it smells really good!"

We're standing in the living room, where there are more knickknacks than I've ever seen in one place. She has hutches, bookshelves, and end tables full of music boxes, tea cups, ceramic and glass figurines, and all kinds of other stuff. It's totally different from our house. My mom can't stand having knickknacks or useless stuff just sitting around.

Dennis must sense my amazement. "Something else, huh? My mom calls them her treasures." He drops his voice to a whisper. "That's not what I would call them."

"Where does she get it all?" I ask.

"The thrift store. Man, she loves that place. There's nothing here that cost more than three ninety-nine. Except maybe the sofa. I think she got that for nineteen ninety-nine."

I look at the old sofa with pink-and-green stripes. She paid $19.99 for that? I think she got robbed. "So, I guess you could call her a treasure hunter?"

He smiles. "Something like that." He picks up a glass penguin as we walk by one of the end tables.

"Help!" he says in a high, squeaky voice. "Get me back to the South Pole. I'm dying here."

"Watch your feet, penguin," I say. "They're not safe around Dennis."

"Wait a second," he says. "Do penguin have feet?"

I give him a shove. "Stop it."

I follow him into the kitchen where his mom is standing at the counter with a spatula, taking cookies off a baking sheet and putting them on a cooling rack. She's a short woman, and has her brown hair up in a bun. She's wearing a bright red-and-yellow apron and a big smile.

"I hope you like chocolate, Sophie."

"I love it," I say.

"Good. This chocolate-chip cookie recipe is our favorite. It's very unique in that the oatmeal is blended before you add it in. Dennis, you want to pour some milk for you two?"

She puts the spatula down and comes over to me, carrying a plate of cookies. "Don't know if you remember me. I'm Margie."

"I remember. We were just talking about his first-grade birthday party."

"Let's see, was that Power Rangers or Spiderman?"

"Power Rangers," Dennis and I say at the same time. Then he says, "I think I still have some action figures around here somewhere, Sophie. You want to play with them when we're done? You could be the pink one."

I raise my eyebrows at him. "I hope you're joking."

Margie hands me the plate of cookies, then turns to Dennis. "You two can use the kitchen table for your homework. I have laundry to put away. Just holler if you need anything, okay?"

"Thanks, Mom."

"Thanks," I echo.

She leaves and we go to the kitchen table. We set the cookies and milk down and drop our backpacks onto the floor. "Let's eat first," Dennis says. "I'm starving."

I take a bite of a cookie. "These are really good."

"Whenever I have someone come over, which isn't very often, Mom makes them. I think it's because they were Michael's favorite."

"Michael O'Reilly?" I ask.

"Yeah. You know we used to be best friends in elementary school, right?"

"You're not friends anymore?" I ask as I reach for my glass of milk.

"Nah. I don't know if you can tell, but I'm not really the athletic type. I tried. I played soccer and baseball through fifth grade. But I just wasn't good enough. It stops being fun when you feel horrible about how you play all the time."

"What does that have to do with being Michael's friend, though?"

He shrugs. "Sports are his life. Things changed. I don't know. Now he hangs out with his friends he sees all the time at games and practices."

He sounds kind of sad. I don't know what to say. He keeps talking. "You and Isabel, you've been friends for a long time, right?"

"Yeah."

He reaches for another cookie. "That's cool. Does she want to be an actress too?"

"No. Flight attendant. Travel the world and all that stuff."

"It's weird," he says. "I always thought girls were the ones who had problems with friends. And here I am, the one with the problems."

I think of the audition and Isabel. I swallow hard. I don't want to go there. "Well, Dennis, maybe if you wouldn't do odd things, like ask people if they want to see a dead bird's foot, you'd have more friends."

His face turns red. "Can I tell you something?"

"Sure."

"I never really had a dead bird's foot."

"You didn't? Then why'd you say you did? Just to freak me out?"

He shrugs. "I don't know. Sometimes I don't know what to say. There was a dead bird on my porch that morning. It just popped into my brain and before I knew it, I was talking crazy-bird-feet talk."

"Well, I guess sometimes I don't know what to say either." I think of the conversation I need to have with Isabel someday about the audition. It makes my stomach hurt just thinking about it. I'm not sure I'll ever figure out what to say for that conversation.

Dennis stands up and takes the empty plate and glasses to the counter. "We should come up with a saying we automatically go to when we're having a hard time. So we don't say something stupid. Like my dad, he always talks about the weather. And he's always so excited about it. Doesn't matter what it is; it can be forty-five degrees and raining, like it is almost every single day in Oregon, and he'll still want to talk about the weather."

"My dad loves the weather too. The Weather Channel is his favorite channel. What is up with that? Look outside, Dad. There's the weather."

Dennis laughs. "I know, it's the truth."

It's quiet for a minute. "We should get to work," I say.

"What's your all-time favorite movie?" he asks.

"I think I'd have to go with *The Wizard of Oz*. Why?"

"No, see, that should be our question. When we don't know what to say. Movies are a safe topic."

"What's wrong with the standard 'How's it going?'"

"Because all you get is an 'Okay' or 'Fine,' and then what? You're right back where you started. It's a useless question. Like anyone is going to tell you how it's really going. 'Hey, thanks for asking. Man, things are terrible. My grandma's sick, my dog just died, and I didn't have any clean underwear this morning.'"

I'm trying hard not to laugh. He's right. It's true. "Come on. Let's get our write-up done. Tell me what you've got for the hypothesis."

He points his pencil at me. "Aren't you going to ask me what my favorite movie is?"

I look at him and smile. "Power Rangers, right?"

He laughs and shakes his head. "You are never going to let me live that down, are you?"

"Nope. Never."

Chapter 11

chocolate pudding

IT CAN SOOTHE EVEN
THE MOST FRAZZLED NERVES

It's Friday, and the audition is still over a week away. As I peek around the corner, waiting for Isabel to leave her locker, I realize I'm being ridiculous. There is no way I can hide from her for an entire week. I'm going to have to tell her. I decide I'll do it at lunch. When she asks me about it, I'll just tell her. Straight out, fast as I can, and it'll be over with. Like ripping off a Band-Aid. She'll be mad. Furious, probably. But I'm going to have to live with it.

I take a deep breath and walk over to our locker.

"There you are," Isabel says. "How's it going?"

I think of Dennis. How he hates that question. And here I am, proof that the question really is useless. Because I can't tell her I'm a mess over this audition thing. Not right now. So I say what I usually say. "Okay. How about you?"

"Dreading that social studies test today. Did you study some more last night?"

"A little bit. I was busy with a science project, though."

She grabs the locker door as I'm about to close it, then takes her lip gloss out of her pocket. She looks in the little mirror we have stuck on the door and moves the wand over her lips.

She turns and smiles. "That's better. Yeah, so I saw you with Dennis Holt yesterday after school. You guys working on something together?"

"Yeah. We have a write-up due today. We got it done yesterday. It actually turned out really good."

"He's kind of different, isn't he?"

"I don't know. I think he's all right. Once you get to know him."

The warning bell rings. "Let's have lunch together, okay?" she says. "I missed you yesterday."

I try to smile. "Yeah, sure. See ya later."

In science, Mr. Leonard gives us a few minutes at the beginning of class to check over our write-ups. We split up into pairs again, and I meet Dennis at his desk this time.

"You want to look it over again?" he asks.

"Not really. But I will."

I take it from him and start reading. "So, big plans for the weekend?" he asks.

"I think I'm watching *Star Wars* with my brother tonight. His first time."

"That is awesome. I still remember the first time I saw the movie. Most amazing thing that's ever happened to me."

I give him a funny look. "You need to get a life, Dennis."

He nods. "I know! You want to help me?"

I look around, wondering if anyone heard him say that to me. "I don't think I can. I have my own problems. Now be quiet so I can read this thing."

He scribbles in his notebook as I finish looking it over. I find one spelling error and make the correction.

"I think it's ready," I tell him. "We did a good job."

"I need a new hobby," he says, still scribbling. "Something fun. I haven't tried anything new since I gave up sports."

"Music?" I ask him.

He shakes his head.

"Martial arts?"

He shakes his head again. "I was thinking something like photography."

"That'd be good."

"I just need a camera."

I sit back in my chair. "Yeah, I'd say that's pretty important if you want to take up photography. Maybe for Christmas?"

He nods. "Yeah. I'll put it on my list."

"Along with your Power Rangers pajamas?"

He gives me an evil grin. "I'm gonna get you one of these days, Sophie. Just you wait."

❀ ❀ ❀

At lunch, Isabel and I find a spot at a table in the corner of the cafeteria. I haven't even sat down and I'm already sweating. My stomach hurts so bad, I didn't take anything from the hot food line. I just grabbed a carton of milk and a bowl of chocolate pudding.

As I sit down, I notice Dennis at a table off to the side, by himself. Does he always sit by himself? I've never noticed before.

"Sophie, what are you doing?" Isabel asks. "You need more than that to eat. You're not on some crazy diet for your audition, are you?"

"No. Just not hungry."

She opens her milk carton, and then pours some dressing on her salad. "Okay, so tell me. Tell me all about the audition. I'm not letting you keep it to yourself one minute longer. I don't care if your agent said you aren't supposed to tell anyone, I am your best friend, and I have to know."

I look over at Dennis. He's reading a book. A book. At lunch! Who does that? The boys down the table from him laugh at someone's joke. Somebody throws a carrot stick across the table. He should be sitting there, having fun. Not alone. What would I do if I didn't have anyone to sit with? If all of a sudden Isabel didn't want to be my friend anymore? Would I be brave enough to go up to a table of girls I don't know very well and ask if I could sit with them? What would I do?

"Sophie?" Isabel says, shaking my arm. "Are you okay? You don't look so good."

I'm breathing fast. I can feel my heart racing. "Um, I don't know."

All I know is I don't want to eat alone. I can't lose Isabel. I just can't.

"The audition is for this new bran cereal," I blurt out. "They want to try to sell it to kids, so they're looking for kids to cast in the commercials. Isn't that the craziest thing you've ever heard? I have to try to get kids to want to eat bran cereal."

She laughs. "Seriously? Bran cereal? Yuck. But if anyone can do it, you can!"

My breathing slows down. I take a bite of my pudding. It tastes good. I take another bite. My stomach feels better. I keep eating.

"So when's the audition?" she asks.

"Monday after Thanksgiving weekend."

"Oh! That's a teacher workday so you won't have to miss school. Too bad, huh?"

I smile and keep eating. I want to dive into this pudding and live there. It reminds me of being little, when a bowl of chocolate pudding made everything better.

Isabel changes the subject then, and starts telling me a funny story about her neighbor, Lana, who's an artist. I'm only half-listening, though, as I watch Dennis get up from the table and leave the cafeteria. Alone.

Chapter 12

candy bars

SO MANY KINDS,
AND EVERYONE HAS A FAVORITE

Dad went all-out on snacks for the big movie night. There's popcorn, lemonade, and various candy bars all laid out on the kitchen counter. Hayden barely eats any of his dinner, he's so excited.

"Couple more bites, Hayden," Mom says. "Or no candy for you."

"Are the spaceships real, Dad?" Hayden asks, before he takes a bite of his hamburger.

"Dude, what do you mean?" I ask. "It's a movie. *Nothing* is real."

"But—"

"Hayden, don't talk with your mouth full," Mom says.

He finishes chewing and swallows. "I mean, did they make spaceships and let the guys fly in them?"

"Let's wait and see what you think, okay?" Dad says. "I don't want to ruin anything for you."

Hayden takes another bite and then jumps up, walks his plate over to the counter, and starts ordering us. "Hurry up, hurry up, hurry up!"

I help Mom clear the table while Dad takes Hayden into the other room.

"I think you should have given him the movies for Christmas, Mom. How are you ever going to top this?"

She takes a sponge to the kitchen table. "Honey, have you been in the toy aisle recently? Something tells me many *Star Wars* products are in our future.

I'm pretty sure this is only the beginning."

"Geez, don't sound so depressed. It could be worse." I start to throw out a joke about Power Rangers, but she probably wouldn't get it.

The phone rings, and I answer it.

"Hey, Sophie, it's Lily."

"Hey. How are you?"

"Really good. I wanted to see if we could get together tomorrow. Maybe go for cupcakes when the shop is actually open?"

"Uh, sure, we could do that," I say. "You want to come over here and we can walk again? We can hang out here for a while too, if you want."

"Yeah, that sounds good. What time should I have my mom drop me off?"

"How about after lunch, like one o'clock?"

"Sounds good. See you then, Soph."

"Bye."

"Was that Isabel?" Mom asks.

"No, actually, it was Lily. She's coming over tomorrow."

"Mom! Sophie!" Hayden yells from the other room. "Come on, it's starting!"

"I'm glad she called," Mom says. "It'll be fun to see her again."

"Come on," I say. "The galaxy far, far away is waiting for us."

"Yes, it is."

Hayden hardly says a word the first half of the movie. Not only that, he hardly moves. He takes a bite of a candy bar when Dad hands him one, and then puts it in his lap, totally forgotten. Normally the kid would have had that thing eaten in ten seconds flat. It's like he's hypnotized. Or maybe he's under the control of the Force.

During one of the battles, my mind drifts to Isabel and how I totally failed as a friend. Her = good. Me = evil. I should wear a Darth Vader costume to school next week for punishment. I'm sure Dennis would love that.

Or maybe I should cancel the audition.

I should.

I really should.

"Mom, will you help me get the popcorn and drinks?" I ask.

I go to the fridge and grab the lemonade. Mom

plugs the air popper in and pours in the kernels. It's noisy. I wait until it's done, and then I tell her about my decision.

"I've decided I don't want to go to the audition," I tell her.

She turns from the stove, where she's melting butter, and looks at me. "What? Why?"

"I can't tell Isabel, Mom. I just can't. I tried today, and I failed. It was horrible."

"Oh, honey. I'm sorry this is stressing you out." She drizzles the melted butter over the big bowl of popcorn. "Why don't you think on it over the weekend. Maybe talk to Lily about it tomorrow, see what she thinks."

"I don't know—"

"We can't call Candace until Monday anyway," she says. "So wait. Sleep on it some more. I really think it's an incredible opportunity, and I'd hate to see you regret it someday."

She hands me the popcorn. "Did you salt it?" I ask.

"Nope. That's your job. I always do too much or too little."

I walk over to the table, grab the salt shaker, and give it four good shakes. Mom reaches in, takes a handful, and pops some into her mouth.

"Perfect."

Well, at least I can do one thing right.

Chapter 13

rocky road cupcakes

THEY PROVE A LESS-THAN-SMOOTH
ROAD ISN'T ALWAYS A BAD THING

The next morning, it is all *Star Wars* all the time, because Hayden won't stop talking about it and can't wait to watch the next one. Mom finally gives in, so I spend most of the morning in my room, watching musicals. I doodle in my dream notebook while I do.

Dream #5—
I dream of wearing beautiful
shoes in a movie one day.
I wonder if Judy Garland
felt like the luckiest girl in the world
wearing those ruby slippers.

At noon, I make a peanut butter and jelly sandwich and slice up an apple before I jump in the shower. Lily arrives right on time.

"Lily, which Jedi is your favorite?" Hayden asks.

"Hayden. Please stop," I tell him. "Not everyone wants to talk space stuff, okay?"

"I like the short green guy," Lily says. She pretends to be thinking. "What is his name?"

"Yoda!" Hayden yells.

"You ready to go?" I ask her. I look out the front window. "Is it very cold?"

"Yeah, it is."

"Okay, let me get my heavy coat."

"Hey, Lily, did you know Sophie's going to be an actress someday?" I hear Hayden saying. "Maybe someone will see her on TV and put her in a movie.

Maybe it'll be a movie with spaceships!"

I walk back out and Lily looks very confused. Yes, my annoying brother will do that to a person. "I'll explain on the way."

Mom comes and says hi to Lily. "We're going to get a cupcake," I tell her.

"Okay, have fun, girls. Call if you decide you want a ride home."

We step outside and it really feels like winter, with the chilly air and the trees almost bare. I zip up my coat.

"Sophie, what did he mean, 'see you on TV'?"

We walk down the front pathway to the sidewalk. I take a deep breath and tell her all about my new agent and the audition.

"That is so exciting!" she says.

"I guess."

She laughs. "You guess? Come on. This could change your whole life!"

"If I tell you the audition is with Beatrice's Brownies, does that change how you feel about it?"

She stops walking, grabs my arm. "No way."

"Yes. Way."

Her face looks almost as pained as my insides have felt these past few days. We continue walking. "What are you going to do?"

"I think I'm going to call my agent on Monday and cancel. I tried to tell Isabel about it last week, but I couldn't do it."

We turn the corner and a blast of cold air comes at us. We walk faster. "What do your parents think?"

"It's crazy. They both think I should do it. It's a great opportunity, Isabel would understand, blah, blah, blah. But what if my commercial was the one to bring their cupcake business down? I would have to live with that for the rest of my life. And maybe without Isabel, which would be even worse."

She looks at me as she holds her coat collar up around her face, trying to keep the cold air away. "But it wouldn't be *your* commercial. You'd be *in* the commercial, but it's Beatrice's commercial. And besides, you might not even get the part. If I were you, I'd go, and think of it as practice for the next audition. I mean, no offense, but I bet not many people get the job from the first audition anyway. It's really competitive!"

"So you'd go to the audition and not tell Isabel who it's with? Just keep it to yourself?"

She shrugs. "Yeah. I mean, a practice audition is not a bad thing. It's not going to hurt anyone."

Hearing her say this fills me with relief. "The only thing is that Isabel knows about the audition. She was at my house when I got the call. I made up excuses as long as I could, but finally on Friday, she said I had to tell her about it. So I lied. I told her it was an audition for bran cereal." I hit my head with my hand. "I can't believe I said that. I wish I could have just told her."

Lily doesn't say anything else. We just walk, our hands tucked into our coat pockets, and our faces buried in our coats as much as possible.

When we reach the cupcake shop, Lily turns to me before opening the door. "Do the audition and then tell her. My mom always says, one thing at a time. That's what you need to do. Right now, focus on the audition and get that over with. When it's all over, you can come clean to Isabel. I mean, what are the chances that the first audition you get called for is their cupcake shop's biggest competitor? It's so crazy it's almost funny. I bet you guys will laugh about it."

She's made me feel so much better. I'm not an evil person. I'm not! No Darth Vader costume for me after all. "Thanks, Lily." I open the door, and the little bell above it rings. "Come on, let's go eat."

We step in, and the first thing I notice is how empty the place is. We're the only ones here.

Isabel's mom, Caroline, walks up to the counter. "Sophie! What a wonderful surprise!"

"Hi! How are you?"

She waves her hand around. "I'd be better if I had a few more customers. But we're fine. Happy about Isabel's win, of course."

I nod and catch Lily out of the corner of my eye, scanning the case of cupcakes. "Oh, this is my friend Lily. We went to theater camp together."

Caroline smiles at Lily. "Nice to meet you. Is this your first time at our shop?"

"Yes. And they all look so good. It's going to be hard to decide."

She lists the flavors, pointing to each one in the case as she does, but I don't hear anything past the first one: Rocky Road. I know instantly, as soon as she says it, that's the one I want.

While Lily tries to decide which flavor she wants, Caroline looks back at me. "Would you like me to call Isabel? See if she wants to come down and sit with you girls?"

For some reason, the thought of seeing Isabel in this empty cupcake shop makes me squirm a little bit. "Um, I think we're actually going to get the cupcakes to go. Right, Lily?"

She gives me a strange look, because that wasn't really the plan. "Oh yeah, right."

"We have stuff to do at home," I explain. "But tell her I said hi, okay?"

She smiles. "Sure will." She turns to Lily. "Okay, what'd you decide?"

"I'm going to try the Raspberry Dazzle. It sounds delicious."

Caroline grabs a pair of black tongs and a little box and reaches into the case to get one of the raspberry cupcakes. I wonder what they do with the ones they don't sell. Do they throw all of them away? It makes my chest ache just thinking about all of those beautiful cupcakes going to waste.

"We'll need a bigger box," I tell Caroline as I reach into my coat to get my wallet. "I want to take home one of each kind."

There goes all of my allowance, which I was going to use for Christmas shopping the day after Thanksgiving. Hopefully I can convince my mom to pay me back. I mean, I couldn't go home with only two cupcakes, could I? That'd be totally rude. And how am I supposed to know what flavor they might like?

One of each is the only solution.

And I sure am good at talking myself into things.

Chapter 14

old-fashioned chocolate cream pie

NOTHING BEATS IT

The week of Thanksgiving all the kids are ready for a break from school, while the teachers make it their mission to cram five days of learning into three. By Wednesday, I'm ready to eat turkey and mashed potatoes until I can't move, lie around, and do nothing all weekend.

First period, I'm counting the hours until the final bell rings.

"Okay, class," Mr. Leonard says as the bell rings, "I'm going to pass your gum experiment papers back to you now. Please pair up with your partner, so you can see my comments and discuss what you might do differently next time. I'd also like everyone to write a paragraph or two about what you liked and didn't like about this particular experiment. It's due at the end of class, please."

Dennis comes over and sits down.

"Think we got an A?" he asks.

"I hope so. Otherwise, you're in trouble."

He laughs. "Me? Why is it my fault? Wait, if we get an A, is that my fault too?"

"Absolutely not."

"You are funny, Sophie Wright. I wish you were a boy."

I start to ask why, but then I think of him eating alone.

"Do you always eat by yourself at lunch?" I ask.

He looks down. Oh no. I've embarrassed him. I

instantly feel bad and wish I could

"Yeah. Most of the time."

"Ever since you've been in midd

He looks back at me. "No. See,
Hikaru were friends. Did you kn
cool. But over the summer, his fam

Now I get it. First he lost Micha
Hikaru. He's lost two good friends t
That's tough.

Mr. Leonard steps up to our d
Sophie and Dennis. You did do you
Mr. Holt?"

I jump in before Dennis has a ch
both did the work. He did as much
even more."

"I'm glad to hear it."

He puts the paper on our desk
minus.

"I should be partners with you
Dennis says. "I've never gotten anyth
a B in this class."

I grab the paper and start flipp
reading Mr. Leonard's comments.

"Oh, before I forget," Dennis says, "I brought you something."

I look up. He reaches into his binder and pulls out a movie. "I thought you might want to watch this. It's really good. You can watch it for research, you know? Since you want to be an actress."

I take the movie and read the title on the case: *Bridge to Terabithia*.

"Isn't there a book with that title?" I ask.

"Yeah. I'm reading it right now. My mom bought the movie the other day, because it was on the five-dollar rack. She asked me if I wanted to watch it with her, so I did, and while we were watching it I thought, *I bet Sophie would like this movie.*"

I smile. "Well, it's better than a bird's foot, that's for sure. Thanks, Dennis. I'm curious to see if I'll like it as much as you think I'll like it."

"You will," he says confidently. "You'll like Jess and Leslie, I know you will."

"Okay, kids," Mr. Leonard says. "Get to work on those paragraphs. Or I'm calling your parents and telling them no pumpkin pie or chocolate cream for you. Only mincemeat!"

The whole crowd groans. Dennis leans in and whispers, "I like mincemeat."

I shake my head. Oh, Dennis.

I sneak my dream notebook out of my binder and quickly write down another dream.

Dream #6—
I dream that Dennis will make
new friends. Besides me.
Yes, this is me actually admitting
I'm Dennis Holt's friend.

I think of Dennis as I stare at the table of pies at my aunt Georgina's house. There's the traditional pumpkin and mincemeat, both of which my grandma loves. I stare at the mincemeat and wonder if Dennis was joking about liking it. It looks pretty disgusting. Do I dare try it? No. Maybe next year. Or maybe never. Mom brought an apple pie, because that's Dad's favorite. And then for the kids, there's chocolate cream and banana cream.

Some of the adults are going back for seconds on the turkey and side dishes. But not the kids. We're ready for dessert. There are seven of us, five boys and two girls. All of the boys are in front of me, getting their pieces of pie so they can finish eating and get the annual football game started in the backyard. My uncle Pete, who's athletic and played football in college, is standing in front of me, trying to keep the boys from rushing the pies and tackling them to the ground.

"Uncle Pete, how long do we have to let our food digest before we can start the game?" Hayden asks him.

"Probably an hour." He turns to me. "You want to join us this year, Sophie?"

Before I can answer, Hayden jumps in. "She's too much of a girl. A girl who's gonna be in a commercial and wants to make sure she doesn't mess up her hair." He puts one hand on his hip and the other hand next to his head where he pretends to fluff up his buzz cut. I give him a nice, girlie shove.

"A commercial?" Pete asks. "Really?"

"Uh, well, no." I glare at Hayden. "I just have an audition on Monday. I'm sure there will be a ton of people there and I won't get it."

"Oh, come on!" he says. "Think positively. You've got to believe it to achieve it!"

Yeah, that's Uncle Pete for you. He's the training manager at a car dealership in town and he's always telling the salesmen that the key to selling cars is to visualize the sales and all this other hocus-pocus stuff.

"Well, I did that for the baking contest and it didn't exactly work out too well for me," I say. "Besides, I'm not sure I want to do commercials anyway. I mean, maybe I should wait. Hold out for a spot on a television show, you know?"

"Don't ever pass up an opportunity, Sophie," he says as he helps Hayden dish up a big piece of chocolate cream pie and put it on his plate. "You never know when another one will come along again. Because many times, they never do. Trust me. If you have a good opportunity, you have to go for it. Or, I promise, you'll regret it later."

Geez, has he been hiding in our closets, listening to my mom?

Oh yeah, that's right. They're brother and sister. Same gene pool and all of that. No wonder.

Chapter 15

monster cookies
THEY'RE NOT SCARY, ONLY DELICIOUS

Jn the car on the way home, Hayden is talking
and talking and *talking* about how much fun the
football game was. Dad, Uncle Pete, and Uncle Ben
played too, and Hayden ended up on Dad's team.
Dad let him play quarterback for part of the game.
Hayden has never been offered that position before
this year. And one of his passes led to a touchdown,
which Hayden cannot shut up about.

I turn and look out the window. We're at a stoplight next to the library, which is completely dark, since it's a holiday. I think of Isabel and all the time she spends at the library, looking at books and dreaming of the places she wants to travel.

Isabel understands dreams. I know that. So why am I having such a hard time telling her? Why can't I tell her about this fantastic opportunity that's been handed to me like a pretty platter of cupcakes—even though it may be for her main competitor?

All my life, I've gone after what I've wanted. That's what I do. When I wanted a dog, I looked and looked until I found one that wouldn't make my mom itch and sneeze. If I hadn't done that, where would we be now? Daisy is what inspired Mom to start her business. The Pampered Pooch wouldn't exist, and our lives would be totally different now. All because I wanted something and did my best to make it happen.

But this time, something is holding me back.

Hayden taps my arm. I turn and look at him. He's holding a wishbone. "Make a wish."

"Where'd you get that?" I ask him.

"The chocolate cream pie," he says, his voice full

of sarcasm. "Where do you think I got it? I stole it from the turkey. So go on. Make a wish."

I close my eyes. I start to wish for myself, but it's all so messy, I don't even know where to start. So I wish for the boy who's been on my mind since yesterday. His life is a little less complicated than mine at the moment. *I wish Dennis would make a new friend.*

"When I say three," Hayden says, "start pulling. One, two, three."

When we start pulling, the bone breaks in my favor.

"No fair," Hayden says. "I want a do-over."

"Don't be a sore loser. Besides, you don't need anything anyway, Little Brother Man. You got *Star Wars*, you got a touchdown, what else do you need?"

"What I need is my very own spaceship."

"Well, you know what Uncle Pete says: You've got to believe it to achieve it."

"What's that mean, Sophie?"

I think for a minute. "I'm pretty sure it means no one can really give you what you want except yourself."

I can't sleep. We came home and played Monopoly together. Dad has no mercy when we play that game. He won again, just like the last twenty-six times we've played. After that, I went to bed and read for a while. When I closed the book, I felt tired. And I wanted to get a good night's sleep, because Mom and I are going shopping tomorrow. I love shopping on the day after Thanksgiving—it's one of my favorite days of the year.

But every time I close my eyes, thoughts of cupcakes and brownies swirl around in my brain. I want to stop thinking about it! How come my brain doesn't have an on/off switch?

At midnight, I get up to see if a glass of milk will do the trick. And a cookie. We didn't eat anything after Thanksgiving dinner because everyone was so stuffed, but now, I'm kind of hungry.

I reach into the cookie jar and pull out one of Mom's homemade monster cookies, Hayden's favorite. They're made with peanut butter, oatmeal, chocolate chips, and M&M's. Mmmm, so good. As I'm pouring myself a glass of milk, I hear someone behind me.

"Can't sleep?" Dad asks.

I turn and look at him. "No, I'm sleepwalking. I'm dreaming about eating a cookie with milk. And about some guy who looks like a pirate standing in the kitchen talking to me, wearing an old green robe that looks like it's been around since 1970."

"Ah, okay," he says. "I thought you might be worried about Monday."

I take a bite of my cookie. "I don't know what you're talking about. What's to worry about?"

He takes a seat on the stool next to the counter. "Have you told her yet?"

"No."

"When are you going to do that?"

I grab my glass of milk and take a seat next to him. "I don't know. Probably next week sometime. Hopefully."

He picks up the glass of milk and takes a drink. "It'll be okay. You'll see."

My eyes drift from his face to the green robe he's wearing. There are stains on the shoulders. "What are those?" I ask him, pointing.

He follows my finger. "Those are the places where you and your brother spit up on me."

"Gross! Dad, get yourself a new robe, would ya?"

He pulls me in and kisses my forehead. "No way. It's one of the few reminders I have of when you were cute and cuddly. You'd cry and your mom would nudge me to say that it was my turn. So I'd get up, go to your crib, bring you down here, and give you a bottle. Then I'd rock you, burp you, you'd spit up on me, and then you'd fall asleep."

I give him a funny look. "They do make these things called burp rags, you know."

"I know, but sometimes, I'd forget to have one with me or you'd miss or—"

"Okay, okay! I can't believe we're sitting here talking about spit-up."

He rubs my hair and stands up. "I think you're the one who started it."

I look at him, my pirate of a dad in an old, ugly robe, and I can't help it. I love the guy so much. I stand and give him a big hug. We stand there for a long time, rocking back and forth the tiniest little bit.

I yawn and pull away. "Okay. I think I can sleep now. Thanks, Dad."

"Anytime, sweetheart. You want me to burp you too?"

I laugh. "Nah, I'm good, thanks."

Before I go, I look at him for a second. For some reason, I don't tell him very often, but right now, it feels like I should. "I love you, Dad. You know that, right?"

He nods. "It's always nice to hear it, though. I love you too. Sleep tight, Sophie."

When I get back to my room, I pull out my notebook.

Dream #7—
I dream of good sleep, sweet dreams,
and a good deal on a bathrobe
tomorrow morning.

Chapter 16

hazelnut chocolate-chip scones

A TREAT WORTH STOPPING FOR

Mom and I are at the mall by seven a.m. It's about thirty minutes from Willow, in the next city over called Delaney. The parking lot is already full, and we have to park a long ways away. And so goes Black Friday madness. Socks at half-price and five-dollar toasters obviously get people out of bed.

Even though I'm tired from being up so late, my blood is pumping and I'm excited. Mom paid me back for the cupcakes and gave me another twenty, so I have money to get some of my Christmas shopping done. She said we could also look for a new outfit for me to wear to the audition on Monday. After we had our little talk while making the popcorn Friday night, I never brought it up again. And she didn't either. I'm pretty sure that means I'm going.

"I know what I want to get Dad," I tell her as we walk through the big, glass doors. "Can we split up so I can do some shopping for both of you, and meet up later?"

She checks her watch. "Two hours enough time? Or do you need more?"

I shrug. "That should be enough. So meet back here at nine?"

"Yes." She hands me Dad's phone.

I wave it in her face. "You know, if you got me one of these for Christmas—"

"Yeah, yeah, I know," she interrupts me. "Now, let me show you, my number is programmed in, right here." She shows me how to dial her, and after that, we say good-bye and I'm on my own.

I walk toward Macy's, thinking about what I should get my mom. She's really hard to shop for. She's so practical, it's not even funny. Like one year, Dad bought her a gorgeous pair of diamond earrings, and she made him take them back.

"Let's use that money to buy coats for the kids," she'd said. "They need coats a lot more than I need a pair of earrings."

Yeah, diamonds are definitely out. Or cubic zirconia in my case, since that's all I could afford with the pitiful amount of cash I have.

When I get to the store, I go to the men's department first and find a sales rack with bathrobes. I grab a gray one that looks good and isn't too expensive, and take it to the counter. A teenage guy is behind the register. He's got brown hair with long bangs that practically cover his eyes. He brushes them back when I walk up and put the robe in front of him.

"This isn't for you, is it?" he asks. "This is the men's department, you know."

Oh. My. Gosh. He thinks I'm a total idiot. "No.

Really?" I look around. "Wow, I wouldn't have known, what with all of the men's pajamas, boxer shorts, and black socks. Huh." I give him the evil eye. "It's a gift for my dad."

He smiles. "Oh, okay. Great."

Great.

After I pay the guy, I look around, trying to figure out where to go next for a gift for my mom. I could get her a robe too, except I don't think I have enough money left.

I wander aimlessly around the store, passing the perfume section (definitely not practical), the department that sells, um, underwear (practical, yes, but I'm not picking out something like *that* for my mother), and the purses (no way—totally different tastes in that department).

I wander a long time, but nothing is hitting me as right for Mom. I'm about to give in and buy her a pair of gloves, because you can't get more practical than that, when a woman walks by carrying a cup of coffee from a coffee shop. That's when it hits me: Mom loves tea. Adores it, in fact. Except we don't have a tea shop in Willow, so she buys the bags at the grocery store and every once in a while, she'll comment on how she'd give anything to have a good cup of tea.

I head back out to the mall and find a map of stores, crossing my fingers there's a tea shop in the mall, or maybe a place that sells good tea. Nothing. So I run to the coffee shop and ask the cashier if she knows of something close by. She tells me there's a shop at the far end of the mall called Flynn's Irish Shop, and they carry some really good tea.

I'm on my way there when I pass a camera shop, and it makes me stop. I don't know why, but I go inside. There are so many cameras, all shapes and sizes. *What kind would Dennis want?* I wonder. Something small that would fit in his pocket, or a big one that allows you to use different types of lenses? They all are pretty expensive. I bet his mom will shop at the thrift store and try to find him one for $3.99. A picture of a beat-up old camera with a broken lens pops into my brain. She wouldn't do that to him, would she?

If I had enough money, I'd buy him one. But I don't. There's nothing that costs less than a hundred dollars in here.

"Can I help you?" the man from behind the counter asks me.

"No," I say. "Just looking." I start to turn to leave, but then I change my mind. "Actually, I have a friend who wants a camera for Christmas. What's a good kind for someone my age? Something not too, you know, expensive?"

"Yes. Let me show you."

He comes around and takes me down an aisle, and we stop in front of a red camera that's out on display. He walks me through some of the features, and then I ask him to write the name and model number on a piece of paper. When he hands it to me, I slip it into my purse, thank him, and tell myself I can't forget about it.

After that, I go to Flynn's and buy tea from Mom. I don't have enough money left to get Hayden anything. I'll have to wait and buy his gift with my December allowance. I head back to the meeting place and wait for Mom.

She walks up a few minutes later carrying four big bags. "Wow," I say. "You've been busy. Want to show me what you got?"

She winks. "You know I can't do that. Come on. I'm hungry. Let's get a snack, and then we'll shop for the perfect audition outfit."

We go back to the coffee shop where we order some tea and hazelnut chocolate-chip scones. While we eat, Mom pulls out Hayden's list and looks it over.

"Is there anything that doesn't involve space on there?" I ask her.

"Yes," she says. "Number one on his list is a tarantula."

"No," I say. "No, no, no. You can't do it, Mom."

She laughs. "Don't worry!"

Just as we're about to get up and leave, someone taps me on the shoulder.

I turn around.

"Hey!" Isabel says. Her grandma Dolores is standing behind her, smiling.

"Hi, Suzanne, hello, Sophie," Dolores says. My mom gets up to greet her.

I stand up and give Isabel a hug. Then I point to her bag. "Let me guess. You just couldn't stay away from the year's biggest sock sale, right?"

She laughs. "Um, not exactly. Takes a lot more than cheap socks to get me out of bed early when there's no school. I bought some Christmas presents for Mom and Dad."

I point to my bags. "Yeah, me too."

"What about your audition on Monday? Are you going to get a new outfit to wear? Something that says, 'I love bran cereal and so will you'?"

I gulp and look at my mom. She and Dolores have stopped talking, and are looking at us.

Oh no.

This is bad. Really bad.

Chapter 17

dark chocolate

RESEARCH SAYS IT'S GOOD
FOR YOUR HEALTH IN SMALL DOSES

I hurry up and answer Isabel before my mom has a chance to say anything. "Yeah, we're on our way right now." I pick up my bags and beg my mom with my eyes not to say a word. "Ready to go, Mom?"

"Ready as I'll ever be, I guess."

"Happy shopping, you two," Dolores says. "Be

careful out there. Those discount-hungry people can get a bit rough."

"Bye!" I call as I rush out into the mall.

I walk fast. Superfast. Like lightning-speed fast.

"Sophie," Mom calls. "Wait up, please."

I slow down, but not very much.

When she reaches me, I don't look at her. "Stop. Sophie, please stop walking."

"Mom, come on, a lot of the door-buster sales end at eleven."

She grabs my arm. "I don't care. Stop, please."

And so I do. When I look at her, I see disappointment all over her face. "You lied to her?"

"I told you, Mom, I couldn't tell her."

"It's one thing to be waiting for the right time to say something. It's another thing to lie!" Her voice is firm. And loud.

I look at the people passing us. They throw pity my way, like candy at a parade.

"Mom, can we not do this right now?" I whisper. "Please? It's embarrassing."

She sighs. "Fine. Let's go home. I think we've done enough shopping for today."

"But what about a new outfit?"

She shakes her head. "I'm not going to reward that behavior, Sophie Wright. We're going home. Give me your dad's cell phone, please, before I forget."

I reach into my pocket, but it's not there. I reach into the other one. It's not there, either. Then I frantically check my purse.

"Sophie?" Mom asks.

I check my pockets a second time. But it's gone. How can it be gone? Wouldn't I have heard it hit the ground if I dropped it?

"Where is the phone?" she asks through gritted teeth.

"I don't know," I whisper.

Mom lets out a disgusted groan. In one minute's time, I've gone from big trouble to seriously BIG trouble.

Mom grabs her bags, walks over to a bench, and plops down. She takes her phone out of her purse and pushes some buttons. She looks at me as she puts the phone to her ear. "You better hope a very kind soul is the one who found it."

She doesn't have any idea.

I stand there and wait, my fate in the hand of some stranger.

"Hello?" Mom says. "Yes, we lost the phone you're holding right now. Are you in the mall?" She listens. "Perfect. We'll be right there. Thank you so much."

She gets up and doesn't say a word. I follow her. We walk through the crowds of people, back toward the end of the mall where the Irish shop is. If I lost it there, she'll want to know what I was doing in that shop. I guess I'd have to tell her, because even a little white lie for the sake of Christmas secrets doesn't seem like a good idea right now.

But instead of the Irish shop, she turns into the camera store.

A short kid wearing a shirt that says PARTLY CLOUDY WITH A CHANCE OF NINJAS is standing at the counter with a petite woman. They're talking to the man who answered my camera questions earlier. I look at the kid hard. He looks familiar.

The salesman smiles and holds out the phone. "So you're the one who dropped it."

"Thank you," I say. "That was almost an epic disaster."

"No problem," he says. Mom steps up and takes the phone from him, and says something I can't hear.

Then the boy says, "Sophie?"

"Yeah."

"I'm Austen. We go to the same school. I have science with your friend, Isabel."

"Hey, I thought you looked familiar. Are you shopping for a camera?"

"Giving my mom some Christmas ideas."

I look at him again, trying to remember something about him. Like who he hangs out with or something like that.

"Wait, are you new at our school?" I ask.

"Yeah. We just moved to Willow last month."

When he says that, the wheels in my head start turning. "Do you know Dennis Holt?" I ask him.

He shakes his head. "The name sounds familiar. He might be in one of my classes, I'm not sure."

"I want to introduce you next week." I look at his shirt. "I think you guys might get along. He likes photography too."

He shrugs. "Okay."

We tell the salesman thanks one more time and then we head home. Mom doesn't say a word to me the whole way.

When I get home, I go to my room and shove Mom and Dad's presents into my closet. Then I grab my dream notebook.

Dream #7—
I dream of a mother
who is not mad at me.

I walk back out to the kitchen and get a square of Mom's favorite dark chocolate, wrap it up in a paper towel, and grab a note card from the little desk in the kitchen. Inside the card I write:

Dear Mom,
I'm sorry about lying to Isabel. I promise I'm going to tell her the truth. I want to get the audition over with so I only have one thing to worry about. Then I'm going to tell her everything. I really hope she

isn't mad at me, although now I guess
I deserve it if she is.

I know what I did was wrong. I
was just so worried about making her
mad, especially because their cupcake
shop isn't doing very well. I'm really
sorry. Please forgive me. You always say,
chocolate makes everything better.
Right now, I really hope it does.

Love, Sophie

Mom's in the other room, curled up on the couch, watching a decorating show on television. I drop the card and the chocolate in her lap, and then I go back to my room, where I stay for the rest of the afternoon.

Chapter 18

peanut butter chocolate-chip granola bars

A DELICIOUS, PORTABLE SNACK

J am so glad when Monday finally arrives, I almost kiss the calendar. It'll feel good to get the audition over with so I can get on with my life. Since last night, I've had what my dad calls "haunted-house stomach." It's that feeling you get when you're about to do something both exciting and terrifying. Who knew stepping in front of a television camera would feel just like walking into a haunted house?

I shower, blow dry and curl my hair, and then put on outfit number twenty-one. That is, last night I tried on about twenty-one outfits before I finally decided on this one. It's a black skirt with a light-blue sweater along with my favorite necklace. Grandma gave it to me last year for my birthday. It's a long silver chain with a big, puffy heart hanging from the end of it.

After I'm dressed and have looked in the mirror enough times to make myself sick of me, I go out to the kitchen where oatmeal with blueberries is waiting for me at the kitchen table.

"You look beautiful, Sophie," Mom says. "Are you nervous?"

"Yeah, a little bit."

"Well, try not to worry. You're going to do great."

I eat my oatmeal while she cleans out the dishwasher. When she's finished, she comes and sits down across from me.

"I know this whole thing with Isabel has been

upsetting to you, and I probably didn't help," she says. "But don't think about any of that today. Just do the best you can, and soak up the experience, okay?"

Mom and I already had a long talk about me lying to Isabel. I've promised to tell her this week, and to apologize.

I nod, agreeing to do my best, and I finish my glass of milk. "I'm ready. Can we go?"

She raises her eyebrows before she says, "After you brush your teeth and wipe the milk off the corners of your mouth."

On the way to the bathroom, I run into a sleepy Hayden.

"Break a leg, Sophie," he says. "Why do they say that, anyway? It makes no sense."

"I don't know, Little Brother Man. But thanks. I think."

Soon, we're in the car and on our way to Portland. Mom puts the *Wicked* CD into the CD player and squeezes my leg. "For some inspiration, huh?"

I nod, sit back, close my eyes, and let myself go back to that magical night.

It takes about two hours to get to Portland. Mom pulls off the freeway, drives into downtown, and I look up at the big, tall buildings. It's so different from our cozy town of Willow. Mom finds a spot in a parking garage across the street from the building where the audition is being held.

When we get inside the building, a woman at a reception desk greets us. She asks us to sign in on a piece of paper, and then sends us to the fifth floor. Once there, a woman directs us to a long line of kids and their parents. It's noisy. I check out my competition. There are all kinds of kids here—girls and boys, short and tall, average and beautiful. Most of them look to be about my age. A couple look older, but I'm guessing most of them are in middle school, like me.

We wait. And wait. And wait.

When we finally get to the table, Mom pulls the paperwork out of her purse and hands it to the lady sitting on the other side.

She looks at the paperwork, then looks up at me and smiles. "Hi, Sophie. Welcome to the audition. Here is a page of lines. You'll want to work on memorizing a couple of them so you can say them when it's your turn, okay?"

I take the paper from her and nod. She marks some things on one of the pages Mom gave her, then hands me a large piece of card stock with the number 99 written on it. Does that mean ninety-eight people are auditioning before me? I turn around and look at the line that's formed behind me. There's got to be another thirty people there.

It really hits me how competitive this industry is. If there's this many people here for a simple commercial, what's it like when it's an audition for a TV show or a movie? It must be harder to get an audition at that point. I bet the headshots become a lot more important. I wonder if you have to be exactly what they're looking for, or you don't get called in.

The lady sends us to a large room where everyone is standing or sitting around, waiting to have their number called. Mom finds us two seats in the far corner of the room.

I read through the lines. Some of them sound a little cheesy.

Do you ever wake up in the middle of the night, craving a delicious snack? Head to Beatrice's Brownies now and stock up before the snack attack hits!

There's only one thing that beats the homework blues. Come to Beatrice's Brownies for all of your snacktime needs.

We wait through the sixties and the seventies.

I study the lines.

We wait through the eighties and the nineties.

I keep studying.

The boy sitting next to me has been playing cards for the last hour. Guess he feels like he's got the lines down. I think I do too. Wish I had brought a book to read or something. Who knew this would be worse than waiting at a doctor's office? Except here, we're waiting for a different kind of shot—a shot at making our dreams come true.

"You doing okay?" Mom asks as she reaches over and puts her hand on my bouncing leg. "Not too nervous?"

"I might have been, like an hour ago," I whisper back. "I can't remember. All I know is that I'm starving and I want to get this over with and go eat lunch. What time is it, anyway?"

She pulls back the sleeve of her jacket and holds her watch out so I can see the time. It's almost one o'clock. No wonder I'm so hungry. Luckily, I have the smartest mom in the world. She reaches into her purse and pulls out a granola bar. I look around and see other kids snacking too.

Mom leans in while I'm chewing. "Just remember, honey, they probably have something specific they're looking for. Either you have it or you don't. If you don't, it's nothing personal. You just aren't *the one* this time around. You know what I mean?"

Not really, but I nod anyway. How do they know what they want until they see it? That's why so many kids are here today. I think it's my job to make them think I'm the one. Except maybe I don't want to be the one, which makes the situation ten times more confusing.

I finish the granola bar in no time, and am about to go in search of a drinking fountain, when the woman with the clipboard who keeps coming in and calling numbers yells out, "Number ninety-nine?"

Mom squeezes my hand as I get up. "Good luck," she says.

I mumble a quick "thanks" and then make my way through all the people to the door, and follow the woman down the hall and around the corner.

She leads me into a room with a light-blue cloth hanging at the front of the room. I'm directed to stand in front of the cloth and hold my number up in front of me. There's a cameraman not far away with a real-life television camera. I tell myself to breathe. Just smile and breathe.

The lady with the clipboard says, "After you say your name and the agency you're with, you can put your number down. Then look at the camera and say one of the lines. If you need help, we've put a couple of them on the easels here and here." She points to two big easels on either side of the camera that have large pieces of paper taped to them with lines written in big black marker.

"Okay, action," she says.

"I'm Sophie Wright," I say. "CPE Agency." I put my hand holding the number down by my side, and then I smile really big and say one of the lines I could actually see myself saying in a real commercial.

"Tired of store-bought cookies in your sack

lunch? Stop by Beatrice's Brownies and get the dessert everyone will be *begging* you to trade!"

"One more, please," the woman tells me.

"Come and try a Beatrice's brownie today. After all, Delicious is our middle name!"

"Great," the woman says. "That's all we need."

That's it? What was that, about thirty seconds? She walks over, takes my number, and says someone will be in touch with my agent very soon if I'm one of the kids selected.

"Thank you," I tell her. "I hope I did all right."

She smiles. "You did great."

I leave the room feeling like I can leap the tall buildings in downtown Portland in a single bound.

It's over. I did it!

When I make it back to the waiting room, I stand at the doorway and wave to Mom. She rushes over.

"How'd it go?" she asks as we walk toward the elevator.

I shrug. "I don't know. But she had me read two lines, and I didn't mess up or anything." I look at her. "She said I did great. So I guess it went pretty well."

She puts her arm around my shoulders and gives me a squeeze. "I'm so proud of you, Sophie. Good job. Now let's go find some lunch."

In my best fake-actress voice I say, "And we should stop by Beatrice's Brownies and stock up before the snack attack hits!"

We giggle all the way down to the first floor.

Chapter 19

chocolate
jam tarts

A DESSERT LIKE NOTHING
YOU'VE EVER TASTED

*H*ow'd it go yesterday?" are the first words out of my best friend's mouth.

"It's hard to know," I tell her as I grab my science textbook along with my binder.

"I can't wait to hear about it at lunch," she says.

I pull my lip gloss out of my pocket. "I need to do

something else at lunch today. Can we get together after school? Maybe have a chocolate jam tart, since today's December first?"

"Oh, yeah!" she says. "Sounds fun. Meet you at the bike rack, okay?"

"Okay. Oh, and Is, can you do me a favor? You have science class with a new kid. Austen? Can you tell him to meet me here, at our locker, at the beginning of lunch?"

She gives me a little eyebrow raise, which tells me she's thinking I've got a crush on the guy. "No, it's nothing like that. Long story. Will you tell him?"

She shrugs. "Okay. See ya later." She scurries off to class and I touch up my lip gloss before I close the door and go to science. When I get to class, I go to Dennis's desk. He looks half-asleep. I know the feeling.

I drop a card in an envelope on his desk in front of him. He jumps a little, sits up straight, and reaches for it. Inside the sealed envelope is a note I wrote to his mom telling her that Dennis told me he wants a camera for Christmas. I gave her all of the important information for the red camera, since that's the one the salesman recommended. I'm hoping it will improve his chances of getting a new one versus getting one from the thrift store.

"Can you give that to your mom, please?"

He turns the envelope over and reads "Margie" in my best cursive handwriting.

"Should I be worried?" he asks.

I start to joke with him and tell him of course he should be, but I don't want him to rip it open and read it. "No, I promise, nothing to worry about. Just wanted to say thanks for letting us study at your house and for the delicious cookies." He sticks the card into his binder. "Oh, and I need you to meet me at my locker at lunch, okay? First thing after the bell rings."

He gives me a funny look. "Uh, okay. Sure."

I start to walk to my desk when he asks, "Hey, Sophie, did you watch the movie yet?"

"I forgot it in my locker over the weekend. I'm taking it home tonight, though."

"You better watch it," he says.

"I will, I will! I've just been, um, kind of busy."

If only he knew.

At lunch, Dennis gets to my locker first. "Am I in trouble?" he asks. "Was an A minus just not good enough for you?"

"I think I found a friend for you. So remember—talk about normal stuff, none of that bird-foot stuff, okay?"

He's about to say something when Austen walks up.

"Austen!" I say. "This is my friend Dennis. He likes photography too. Or, at least, he wants a camera for Christmas, like you, so he can get into photography. I thought maybe we could have lunch together?"

Austen turns to Dennis and says, "On Sunday, my dad took me steelhead fishing. I took pictures with his camera when he was gutting one of the fish. Wanna see?"

Dennis looks like he's just been offered a hundred dollar bill. "Yeah!"

Austen pulls some pictures out of the back pocket of his jeans. "Have you ever been steelhead fishing?"

"Nah, just bass fishing. Is it fun?"

They start walking toward the cafeteria, lost in a sea of fishing and photography.

I am so proud of myself.

It's a match made in middle school.

After school, Isabel and I ride our bikes to It's Raining Cupcakes. The sweet smell of baked goods greets us when we walk in the door. Today there's a mom with three little kids sitting in the shop. This makes me very happy.

Isabel's grandma is behind the counter. "Hello, Sophie," she says, wiping her hands on a pink-and-white towel. "I'm glad to see you survived Black Friday."

"Barely," I say. If only she knew I'm not really joking.

"Grandma," Isabel says, "I brought Sophie in to try one of the jam tarts. Can we have two, please? With milk?"

"That's just ducky," she says. "Coming right up."

We stand aside and watch as the mom with the three kids tries desperately to keep the frosting situation from getting out of control. That is, out of their hair, off their clothes, and into their mouths.

"Here you go," Dolores says, handing me my jam

tart and glass of milk. Isabel takes hers, and then we take a seat in the corner.

"Isabel, it looks fantastic," I tell her.

She smiles. "I hope you like it."

"You know I will."

And I do. It's *really* good. The flavor of the strawberry jam with the chocolate tart is like nothing I've ever tasted before. I can see why it won the contest.

Just then the little bell over the door jingles, and Stan walks into the shop. He looks over at us and waves.

"Hello, Isabel!" he says. "Long time, no see. My wife sent me to get some of your jam tarts to try. Seems like we've been waiting forever to get our hands on them." He chuckles. "Or our mouths, as the case may be."

"Thanks, Stan. Did I ever tell you it was those tarts you brought from England that inspired my recipe?"

"No, I don't believe you ever told me that. Isn't that wonderful? I'll have to make sure to tell Judy. She gave me such a hard time about bringing those tarts all the way from England. See, I knew there was a reason why I felt so strongly you should have some."

He orders half a dozen and Isabel's grandma boxes them up for him.

"How's business?" he asks her.

Dolores folds her arms across her chest and sighs. "The last month or two has been very slow. We're hoping things pick up now, with the holidays around the corner. The shop will be open seven days a week in anticipation of all of the holiday parties going on in town. We're featuring some wonderful, special flavors for the season. After you've finished those tarts, you'll have to come back and try some gingerbread cupcakes."

"We'll definitely do that," he says. "Thanks, Dolores. Say, did anyone ever call you Dee growing up?"

"Oh yes," she says. "My little sister couldn't say Dolores for the longest time, so she called me Dee. Even today, I'm Dee to her."

"Knock, knock," Stan says.

"Who's there?"

"Dee."

"Dee who?"

"Dee-licious jam tarts for sale!" he says, holding the box in the air.

She laughs, and he waves good-bye and disappears out the door.

"I love that guy," Isabel says.

"Me too," I say, before I finish off the last of my tart. "Is your mom doing okay, Chickarita? I mean, she isn't too worried about business, is she?"

She stacks our plates and pushes them aside. "I don't know. It's hard to tell with my mom. She's trying really hard to focus on the good stuff—the people who love our shop come here again and again. The hard thing is figuring out unique, inexpensive ways to drum up new business. To get people to come and try a cupcake when they haven't been here before. If only we had an advertising budget as big as Beatrice's. Must be nice to be a big, ugly chain, huh?"

I gulp and take a swig of milk. This is when I should tell her.

Right now.

Right. Now.

And then the door of the shop opens again. I watch as a girl with dark, straight hair comes through the door followed by a pretty woman. The girl turns and looks at us.

I jump up. "Lily!"

She waves and walks over to our table.

"Isabel, this is my friend Lily," I say. "I brought her here last week to try the cupcakes. And look, she's back!"

Lily turns to Isabel. "My mom has book club tonight. I told her she had to buy cupcakes for snacks this time. They're *so* good, I just don't understand how business can be slow for you guys."

"How do you know that?" Isabel asks.

Lily's cheeks start to turn pink, almost matching the fuchsia coat she's wearing. "Uh, I—"

Isabel looks at me, her eyes sad. "Did you tell her? Are you telling people my family's business is having a hard time? That's really personal, Sophie."

I grab her arm. "I know it is. But—"

She shakes her head and pulls away from me. "Look," she whispers, nodding at the people in the shop, "I don't want to talk about this right now. I'm

gonna go upstairs. Call me later if you want to."
She turns to Lily. "I hope your mom's friends like
the cupcakes."

After she leaves, Lily says, "I'm sorry." I can tell
she feels really bad.

I sigh. "Don't worry about it."

I'll worry enough for the both of us.

Chapter 20

chocolate-covered
strawberries

CELEBRATE!

*W*hen I get home, I find Mom working away
at her sewing machine, which is the way it will be for
most of December. Apparently clothing for dogs is
a popular gift item during the holidays. Who knew?

"What are you working on?" I ask as I go to the
fridge and grab a bottle of water. A tray of chocolate-
covered strawberries catches my eye. That's weird.

Those are something you have for a special occasion. Well, maybe they have a party to go to.

"I'm trying to get twenty of these made," she says. I look over and she's holding up a tiny pink shirt that says FRIENDS FUR-EVER.

I laugh. "Oh, Mom, that is classic. Dogs everywhere are going to hate you, you know that, right? Because a true friend would never put a dog in a shirt!"

She takes a pair of scissors and cuts a thread. "Maybe dogs enjoy wearing clothes, Sophie. Have you ever asked Daisy if she might like it? I mean, how do you know her true feelings on the subject?"

I've told my mom that Daisy will never be caught in anything other than the coat she was born with. Once in a while, Mom uses Daisy for a model, but that's it. The clothes go on, she takes a picture, the clothes come off.

"Mom, seriously, you've seen her face when you put something on her. She looks humiliated. Like you would look if someone told you to run across a football field in your underwear in front of millions of people."

"I actually did that once," she says. I practically

choke on my water. "Just kidding. But your dad, he may have really done it. You should ask him."

My family is so weird.

"Well, I'm going to go watch a movie a kid at school loaned me."

"What movie?"

"*Bridge to Terabithia.*"

"I've read the book," Mom says, "but I haven't seen the movie. You'll have to let me know what you think after you watch it. The story centers around friendship. I bet you'll like it. Speaking of friendship, did you tell Isabel today?"

I bring my hands to my face and shake my head.

"Sophie."

I put my hands up, like I'm surrendering. "I know, Mom. I know! I need to tell her. Tomorrow. I'm going to do it tomorrow no matter what. First thing, at our locker." I make an X over my heart. "Cross my heart and all of that. Now can I go watch my movie?"

"Yes."

Dream #8—
Wouldn't it be great if

courage grew on trees,
so if you needed some,
you could just go out
and pick a basketful?

The movie is good. It's kind of slow at first, but after a while, I'm into it. I'm about halfway through when Hayden pokes his head in.

"Mom needs you in the kitchen," he tells me.

Probably wants me to set the table. Why doesn't she have Hayden do it? I hit the pause button with a big sigh.

When I walk into the kitchen, Mom, Dad, and Hayden are standing there holding fancy champagne glasses. A bottle of sparkling cider is on the counter, next to the platter of chocolate-covered strawberries.

"What's going on?" I ask.

"Congratulations!" Mom and Dad call out. Hayden puts the glass to his mouth and chugs it.

Dad hands me my own glass. "I don't get it," I say. "What are you congratulating me for?"

"Your agent called today," Mom says. "I wanted

to wait until your dad got home to tell you. You got the part!"

I feel my knees buckling. I grab the counter, setting the glass of cider down in front of me. "What? Are you serious? That can't be right."

"Would I kid you about something like this? Running through a football field in my underwear is one thing, but your acting career is quite another."

Dad looks at Mom like she's gone insane.

"What did Candace say exactly?"

"She said you are just what they're looking for. On-screen, you look fantastic, like the girl next door, friendly and approachable. They love you, Sophie! They want to film the actual commercial very soon."

Now I look at Mom like she's gone insane. They *love* me? Did she really say that?

"What did you tell her? Did you say I'd do it?"

"Yes, honey, of course I did! You have the chance to be on television, which could lead to other, bigger roles. Who knows how far this could take you? And they'll pay you! You could take that money and buy some lessons, like you've been talking about."

Bigger roles?

Money for acting lessons?

This is so amazing!

And then I think of Isabel. And it's not so amazing anymore. Part of me wants to dance down the street while the other part of me wants to find a hole and crawl in it.

I try to push the thought of bigger roles and money for acting lessons out of my mind. It's like pushing a huge boulder down the street—I have to push really, really hard. Finally, with what feels like a boulder in my throat, I say, "Mom, I don't think I can do it. You should call her back and tell her I can't."

Dad steps forward and puts his arm around me. "Honey, wait a second. Not so fast. Is this about Isabel?"

"Yes," I say. "I won't make her choose between me and her family. I won't. So I have to be the one to make the hard choice."

Dad gently pulls me over to the table and pulls out a chair. I sit down, then he sits down across from me, and Mom does the same.

"Can I go to my room?" Hayden asks, his hands full of chocolate-covered strawberries.

Dad's soft, warm eyes don't move from my face. "Yes, please." He waits until he's gone. "Don't you think you should talk this out with Isabel? See what she says about it? You might be surprised, Sophie."

I shake my head. "Dad, this whole time I've been trying to figure out what made it so hard for me to tell her. And I finally know. I figured it out yesterday when we went to the cupcake shop after school. She cares about her family so much. Things with her mom haven't always been easy, but she loves her! And I'm her best friend, so of course she cares about me too. How can I tell her that I want to do the commercial, but only if she says it's okay? I'd be asking her to make an impossible choice."

"But I don't think—"

I interrupt Mom. "Isabel is one of the nicest people I know. People at school gave her a bad time about winning the contest, and she never got mad. They thought she was buying stuff, being selfish, and what is she doing with the money? Taking *me* on a trip to Seattle. See? Nice! This is my chance to do something nice for Isabel. Don't you understand? I need to make the choice for her."

Dad looks at Mom. "I think it should be Sophie's decision. If she doesn't want to do it, we need to respect that."

I stand up. "Good. I'm not doing the commercial."

Mom comes over and gives me a hug. "Okay. If that's what you want. I'll call Candace first thing in the morning, when the office is open. It's too late now."

"Okay. Can I go back to my room, please?"

Mom nods. "I'll call you when dinner is ready. Should be about twenty minutes."

I look at her. "Please don't. I'm not hungry."

Dream #9—
I dream of more chances.
Please let there be
more chances.

After I write in my dream journal, a gift from the nicest friend in the universe, I think about calling Isabel to apologize for what Lily said.

But I can't. Because I'm too busy crying.

Chapter 21

chocolate-flavored
lip gloss

IT CAN HELP YOU THROUGH THE DAY

J think I got thirty minutes of sleep. Maybe forty. But I am ready to tell Isabel about the audition and now, with me turning down the commercial, I can honestly tell her I did it just for the practice.

I put on my favorite jeans and my favorite black blouse, and while I put on my favorite chocolate cherry lip gloss, I give myself a pep talk in the bathroom.

"You are going to get this thing over with, Sophie Wright. Walk up to her at the locker, tell her you have something to say, and tell her. Get it all out, let her know how sorry you are for lying, but you really didn't want to upset her. Then it's over with. Along with your friendship. And your acting career." I shake my head. "Stop it. It'll be fine."

It'll be fine.

I keep telling myself those three words over and over as I walk to the kitchen. Mom is there, and I swear she looks like the dog has just died. In fact, it makes me wonder. "Where's Daisy?" I call for her. "Daisy? Daisy, come here!"

She comes running from the family room, carrying a rawhide bone in her mouth. I reach down and scoop her up into my arms, leaving the slimy bone on the floor.

"I have some bad news, Sophie," Mom says.

I knew it. "What? Tell me!"

She throws the *Willow Gazette* onto the table. I look down and see a picture of me along with the headline "Local Willow Girl to Star in National Ad Campaign for Beatrice's Brownies."

"What?" I yell so loudly it scares Daisy and she jumps out of my arms. I look at Mom. "How did this happen?"

Mom speaks slowly, like her words are tiptoeing out of her mouth. "I think Candace must have sent out a press release yesterday."

I shake my head. "No. No, no, no, no, no! Mom, wouldn't she talk to me about it first? Make sure I wanted to do the commercial?"

"You went on the audition. I think to her that meant you wanted to do the commercial."

I start pacing, back and forth, back and forth, my mind racing with questions and worries. I check the clock, and then realize I have to talk to Isabel before she sees it. I run to the phone and dial her number, but no one answers.

"Mom, will you drive me to school? Now?"

"Do you want to eat anything first?"

"No. I need to go!"

"Okay, but we have to take Hayden too, and he needs to eat breakfast."

I throw my hands in the air. "Never mind. I can get there faster on my bike."

I run to my room, grab my coat and backpack, and head to the garage. When I open the door, I see it's raining. Perfect. I put my hood up and off I go.

All I can think about the whole way to school, rain pelting my face, is that this is what I get for lying to Isabel. My mother couldn't have put together a better punishment than this if she'd tried.

When I pull up to the bike rack, Isabel is there too, putting her bike into one of the spaces.

I jump off my bike and run over to her. "Isabel, I have to talk to you."

Even with her wet, rain-covered face, I can tell in an instant that she knows. I imagine her and her parents seeing the picture and the headline and looking at one another, stunned. Disgusted. All because of me, the person who is supposed to be Isabel's best friend in the world.

"I don't have anything to say to you," she says, bending down to secure her lock.

"Please, Chickarita, I can explain."

She stands up, her bottom lip quivering, because she's trying so hard not to cry. "You lied to me. You stabbed my family in the back. That pretty much explains it all, doesn't it?" She turns and runs into the school before I can say anything else.

I turn my face to the sky and let the rain pound my face. I don't know what to do now. How can I go in there? If my best friend is mad at me, everyone else will be too. No one will want to hear my side of the story.

I start to head back home, because I feel like there's no where else to go, when Dennis comes running up, the black hood on his hoodie covering his head.

"Sophie, I saw the paper," he says. "Congratulations. You never told me you were doing that. Wait. Why is your bike headed away from school? Where are you going?"

"Home." And as soon as the word is out, I start crying. The warm tears blend in with the cold raindrops, and it feels funny. "I can't believe what a mess I've made." He takes my bike and parks it. Then he walks back to me, takes my hand, and pulls me toward the front steps, which are covered. He sits down and pulls me down next to him. He lets me cry for a few minutes. Then he asks, "Isabel didn't know about the commercial?"

I shake my head. "She knew I was auditioning, but she thought it was for something else." I look at him. I can barely see his eyes behind his wet glasses. It's like he can read my mind, because he takes them off and starts wiping them on his jeans. I never noticed Dennis's eyes before. They're green with little yellow specks around the middle. Different. Nice.

"You lied to her?" he asks.

"I know, I'm horrible." I bite my lip to keep from crying some more. Then I take a deep breath. "I was going to tell her everything today. I swear. And I didn't want to do the commercial. I went to the audition just to see what it was like. But yesterday my mom told my agent I'd do it, even though she hadn't talked to me about it yet."

He puts his glasses back on. "Yep. That's a mess."

He stands and pulls me up with him.

"Where are we going?"

"You're going to lock your bike, and then we're going to science class. You can't run away, Sophie. Everything will still be here tomorrow. And the next day. And the day after that."

"But—"

"Nope. You have to go in. Trust me. You may not have had friend troubles before, but I have."

"Dennis—"

He turns and faces me. "I will be with you whenever I can. Between classes. At lunch. After school. People will leave you alone if you're with me. And we'll figure out a plan to get Isabel to forgive you. I'm going to help you. I promise. Okay?"

I feel like I'm putting my life in Dennis Holt's hands. And for some strange reason, I'm okay with that.

Chapter 22

brownies

A WONDERFUL DESSERT TO SHARE
WITH A FRIEND

Dream #10—
I dream of forgiveness.
Lots and lots of forgiveness.

Somehow with Dennis's help I make it through the morning. I hear kids whispering about me, but I keep my head down and tell myself *It doesn't matter, it doesn't matter, it doesn't matter.* Even though it really does. I remember how I told Isabel I could do something terrible to take the attention off of her and the baking contest. Well, looks like I succeeded.

A couple of teachers congratulate me on the commercial, and one actually hangs the newspaper article in the hallway, outside her door. Dennis asks her to take it down. She does.

Isabel doesn't even look at me in Math or English. I try passing her a note. She rips it up without even reading it.

At lunch, Dennis and Austen walk me through the lunch line. I tell Dennis I don't want anything to eat, but he doesn't listen to me. For lunch I'm having a grilled-cheese sandwich, French fries, apple slices, and a brownie. Guess he wasn't thinking when he picked the brownie for me. I'm pretty sure I'll never want to eat another brownie as long as I live.

When we sit down, I pass it to Austen. He stuffs the whole thing in his mouth and just like that, it's gone. If only I could have him do that with all of my brownie problems.

While I tear my sandwich into pieces, Dennis gives

Austen a quick rundown of what's going on between Isabel and me.

"Can we just talk about movies or something?" I ask. I look at Dennis. "Did you ask him what his favorite movie is, like you're supposed to?"

"Didn't even have to," Dennis says. "If I said something stupid, he just laughed and said something stupid back."

If I wasn't so upset, this would make me very happy.

"You need a plan," Austen says, reaching for my fries because he's already eaten all of his.

"Right," Dennis says. "Something big. Really big."

They start talking about what their favorite super-heroes would do while I scan the cafeteria, looking for Isabel. I don't see her anywhere. I start to get up, but Dennis grabs my arm.

"Where are you going?"

"To find Isabel, so I can talk to her. She needs to hear the whole story. She only knows part of it right now."

"Sit down," he says. "You need to give her a couple of days to cool off."

"And don't do it here at school," Austen says.

"One person will hear you and in five minutes, the whole school will know what you said."

"Plus, they'll throw in things that aren't true," Dennis says. "A five-minute conversation will morph into a thirty-minute fight out on the football field."

I sit back down. They're right. I can't do it here. Maybe I can get her to meet me at the Blue Moon Diner after school. Ha, who am I kidding?

Dennis and Austen are still talking, and now they've turned the fight on the football field into one that includes ninjas and pirates. While they battle it out over who would win, I rack my brain trying to think of what I can do to get Isabel to realize how sorry I am.

Something big.

Something eye-catching.

Something really, really awesome.

I wish I could hire a television crew and pay for advertising. I'd put the best commercial ever on television. But that costs thousands of dollars and after spending all of my money on Christmas gifts, I don't even have five dollars in my wallet.

But I keep rolling that idea around in my head,

and it gets bigger and bigger, like a snowball rolling down a hill. Pretty soon my head is so full of this idea, I can hardly see straight.

"No, see," Dennis is saying, "the pirates would bring their cannons and—"

"I know what to do. I'm going to dress up like a cupcake."

They both turn and look at me like I just said there are no such things as pirates and ninjas.

"What do you mean?" Austen asks. "Frosting is really messy. I think it'd be hard to wash out of your hair."

"No, not a real cupcake. A pretend cupcake. Can you guys help me? I think we'll need to make a trip to the craft store."

"What's a craft store?" Dennis asks as he straightens his glasses.

I put my head in my hands while Austen and Dennis laugh over the idea that there are actual stores that sell craft-making supplies.

Boys.

My mom said one time, "Can't live with them, can't live without them." I'm pretty sure now I know what she meant.

Chapter 23

ice-cream
sandwiches

THEY'RE EASY TO MAKE AND YUMMY

Saturday morning, I wake up to rain pounding the roof. In my nightmare, it was Isabel pounding on my window, yelling, "You're the worst friend ever! Worst. Friend. Ever!"

I make myself open my eyes, and I go to my window. The sky is a dark, dark gray and the trees are blowing left, then right, then left again, the wind whipping them around like puppets.

I plop back on my bed, pull the covers over my head, and decide I will just stay there forever. But eventually, my bladder overrules my decision. As much as I love my bed, I don't love it *that* much.

I run into Mom in the hallway. "Any big plans for today?" she asks.

"I was thinking about staying in bed forever. But since I'm up, could you take me to the craft store later? And give me an advance on my allowance? I have some things I need to pick up. My friends Dennis and Austen are going to help me. Is it okay if they come over here this afternoon?"

"Sure. That's fine."

I slip past her and use the bathroom, then go back to my room. Mom comes in a little while later with a plate of toast and a cup of orange juice. She takes a seat on the chair that sits by my desk. She's been really great, leaving me alone like I've asked the past few days. I haven't wanted to talk about it. But I guess the time has come.

"I'm assuming you haven't talked to Isabel yet," she says. "When are you planning on doing that?"

I set the juice on my nightstand. "Mom, she is so mad. She avoided me at school all week like she'd break out with some terrible disease if she even looked at me. I tried writing her notes. I tried talking to her at our locker. She didn't want anything to do with any of it."

Mom sighs. "You girls are so dramatic, you know that?"

"I'm an actress," I tell her. "Drama is my specialty."

"And apparently Isabel's too. Honey, I have faith that you girls will work this out. I think you just have to keep trying. She can't ignore you forever."

I nod. I hope this plan I have works.

"Mom, do you think Isabel is mad that the commercial is with Beatrice's Brownies? Or is she mad about me not telling her the truth?"

"Have you finished watching that movie your friend loaned you?" she asks.

"Not yet."

"Well, I don't want to give anything away, but you should finish watching it. And think about what makes Jess and Leslie's friendship so strong. They want to help each other find their true selves. To celebrate that which is special about each of them. Don't you think Isabel wants that for you, Sophie, just like you want it for her?"

"I don't know," I tell her.

Mom pats my leg and then gets up to leave. "I think you do."

*Dream #11—
I dream
my plan will work.*

I call Dennis and tell him to be at the craft store at one o'clock. He says he'll call Austen and let him know to meet us there too.

When I get there, Dennis and Austen are waiting for me by a big display of papier-mâché reindeer. They each have two reindeer in their hands.

"So here's our plan," Austen says in a deep voice with a funny accent. "We wait until Santa isn't looking. Then we grab all of the video games."

"And comic books," Dennis says, trying to copy Austen's weird reindeer voice. "Don't forget the comic books."

"Like you can do that with four hooves," I say as I take the reindeer away from Dennis and put them back on the display. "Come on. We have some shopping to do."

I grab a cart and we begin strolling the aisles of the store. Shopping in a craft store is pretty entertaining with two boys. Every aisle, they have something new to say about what they see.

"So this is where cemeteries get all those fake flowers."

"Was my grandma just here? This place smells like her house."

"Everything better be half-off, since everything's only half put-together."

"What's a hot-melt glue gun? Sounds like a torture device for aliens."

"Boys," I say. "Focus. Giant cupcake. Remember?"

"Right," Dennis says. "Hey, I sketched out an idea last night. We need a big, round laundry basket, though. Do you have one at your house?"

"Yeah," I say, "we do. Why?"

"Think your mom will mind if we cut the bottom out of it?"

Dennis pulls a piece of paper out of his pocket and shows me the design. It is perfect. Genius! It's so good, I almost want to kiss him. Almost.

The laundry basket will be the bottom half of the cupcake. We'll wrap it in something to make it look like a cupcake wrapper, then we'll put a whole bunch of fabric on the top, and sort of puff it out somehow, to make it look like lots of frosting. To wear the costume, I'll have to attach straps to the laundry basket. Then I'll step into the basket with my feet, pull it up to my hips, put the straps over my shoulders, and suddenly I'm a walking, talking cupcake.

We go to work filling the shopping cart with the supplies we need. When we go to the cash register, our cart holds three rolls of aluminum foil, a pink fleece blanket, cardboard, some purple and red felt, a roll of pink ribbon, a Styrofoam ball, red spray paint, glue, thick masking tape, and a big poster board.

After I pay for the stuff, Mom is in the parking lot waiting for us, and she helps me put the bags in the trunk of the car. The boys get in the back and I sit up front with my mom.

"You want to tell me what you kids are up to?" Mom asks.

"Sorry, ma'am," Dennis says. "Top-secret operation."

"Yes, and our top-secret operation requires a round laundry basket," Austen says. "We understand you have one. Could we use it, please? We won't be able to give it back, since we have interesting things planned. But don't worry. Nothing illegal."

I watch as Mom looks in the rearview mirror, smiling. "You want my laundry basket? It's full of laundry, you know."

"If we do the laundry, can we have the basket?" Dennis asks.

Mom looks at me. "Sophie, I like these boys."

When we get home, we go into the garage and get to work on what is now called "Operation Cupcake." Never has making a cupcake been so important.

We have so much fun, and I can't stop laughing. They don't settle for good or okay. If I say, "That looks okay," they start over and try again. Everything has to be over-the-top, out of this world, amazing. And when the whole thing is done, that's exactly what it is.

The laundry basket is covered in silver foil. The fleece blanket is rolled and puffed out on top of the laundry basket, with a little bit of help from some cardboard. Hearts made out of red and purple felt are glued all over the pink fleece, like pink and red sprinkles. The Styrofoam ball is bright red, and has a stick poking out the top, which Dennis got from our yard. The red ball is glued to a pink ski hat I found in my closet. Yes, the walking, talking cupcake will even have a cherry on top. I decide that tomorrow, when I put Operation Cupcake into play, I'll wear some pink tights and old ballet slippers to complete the look.

After a couple of hours, Mom brings us a plate of homemade ice-cream sandwiches—a scoop of chocolate ice cream between two oatmeal cookies. When she sees me in the costume, she almost drops the plate.

"What do you think?" I ask, twirling around for her.

"I think you are the cutest cupcake I've ever seen!"

I hold up the poster board and show her the sign I've made that I'll carry tomorrow.

BUY A CUPCAKE
AT IT'S RAINING CUPCAKES
AND TELL THEM SOPHIE
SENT YOU!

"Operation Cupcake is complete," Dennis says.

"Good," Austen says. "Because my stomach is telling me it's time for Operation Ice-Cream Sandwich."

I go over to my mom and tell her thanks for the snack. "Operation Cupcake is a great idea," she tells me.

"I just hope it works, Mom."

She reaches for my hand and gives it a little squeeze. "It looks like a winning recipe to me."

Chapter 24

cherry cupcakes

DRIZZLE THEM WITH WHITE CHOCOLATE
TO SHOW YOUR LOVE

*J*t's Sunday afternoon. Time to put Operation Cupcake into action.

Dennis called earlier and gave me a pep talk. It went something like this:

"You have to be the best cupcake that's ever walked the face of the earth."

"And how exactly do I do that?" I asked him.

"I don't know," he said. "But something will come to you."

"Hey, Dennis?"

"Yeah?"

"Remember how you said you were going to get me for bringing up the Power Rangers? Operation Cupcake isn't going to show up in the school newspaper tomorrow, is it?"

"You know, that's not a bad idea." He paused. "Just kidding. You have nothing to worry about, I promise. I just want things to be better with Isabel."

"Yeah. Me too."

He might not have been as motivational as Uncle Pete would have been, but he was all right. And I'm ready to do what I have to do. Mom drops me off around the corner from It's Raining Cupcakes. Before I get out of the car, she says, "Good luck, honey. Remember to speak from your heart."

If she gives me the chance to speak at all. "Okay. Thanks, Mom."

"What time should I pick you up?" she asks.

"I can walk home."

She hands me her phone. "Take this, just in case. And don't lose it!"

I slip it into the pocket of the shorts I'm wearing over my tights. I get out of the car, pull the costume and sign out of the backseat, and slip the costume on. Mom waves good-bye and pulls away. I suddenly wish I had asked Dennis to come with me. No, that wouldn't have been right. I have to do this by myself. This is about me and Isabel, and I have to show her I'll do whatever it takes to make things right between us.

With my cherry-topped hat in place and the sign in front of me, I begin walking up and down the sidewalk. I do this for probably thirty minutes, back and forth, from one end of the sidewalk to the other. But then I realize I'll have more visibility if I increase the size of the area I'm covering.

So I broaden my path. I go across the street and make a big loop. Around the bookstore, past the post office, past the big park where some kids are playing, and back around to the cupcake shop.

After an hour of doing this, my legs are starting to get tired of walking and my shoulders are sore from the straps holding up my costume. Still, I'm not ready to give up. I create an even bigger loop. With every route, I make sure that I pass by the cupcake shop at some point.

Cars drive by and honk, and I wave, and soon I notice that traffic has increased a lot in front of the shop, and I see person after person going into the store and coming out with their boxes of cupcakes.

It's working.

People are buying cupcakes!

And so it goes, hour after hour, until every muscle in my body aches and I've waved at so many cars, my arm feels like it's going to fall off.

And yet, not one sign of Isabel.

A raindrop falls, and then another one, and soon it's not just sprinkling, it's outright pouring. My stomach, as well as the darkened sky, tells me it's time to go home. Four hours of total humiliation must not have been enough to show Isabel how sorry I am.

I thought she'd realize how bad I feel.

I thought she'd come see me, tell me it's okay, and that I'm forgiven.

It wasn't enough.

Obviously, there's still more I have to do.

Maybe it's what Dad said to me that one night I couldn't sleep. Sometimes you know how someone feels, but it's nice to hear it too.

I walk to the side of a building and stand underneath the awning, to stay dry. I take the phone out of my pocket and dial Isabel's number.

"Hello?"

"Isabel, it's me, Sophie. Please don't hang up. Look, maybe it's not going to make much difference, but I want you to know how sorry I am that I lied to you about the audition. I didn't want to make you choose between me and your family. I never planned on actually doing the commercial. I went to the audition for practice. But then my agent called, and my mom was so excited, and neither of them asked me if I wanted to do the commercial. And I don't! If it means losing you as a friend, I don't want to do it. I'm not doing it. Isabel, you have to believe me. I'm so sorry."

She doesn't say anything for a long time. And then finally, she lets out a sigh and says, "Okay. Thanks for calling." And she hangs up.

I stand there, watching the rain fall. It's definitely not raining cupcakes.

As if the day hasn't been bad enough, now I get to walk home in the rain. Perfect. Just perfect.

I've about reached the corner when I hear a voice.

"Hey! Sophie Bird!"

I turn around and there's Isabel. She gives me a little wave.

I try to run, but laundry baskets aren't really made to run in. So I walk, really, really fast. When I reach her, she pulls me under the awning of Stan's barber shop.

"How is it possible that you look so amazing and so ridiculous all at the same time?" she asks.

"Takes a special talent," I say.

"You got that right. What kind of cupcake are you, anyway?"

"Cherry and white chocolate. It's a special creation, just for you. I hope you like it."

She pauses, and then says, "You shouldn't have lied to me."

"I know." I start to cry. "I'm so sorry. I handled it all really badly, and I want to talk to you about it some more. Can we go upstairs, to your place?"

She looks at me. "Under one condition."

"Anything."

"That you do the commercial."

"But—"

She shakes her head. "It's a chance of a lifetime, Soph! You have to do it. Whatever happens to the cupcake shop is going to happen whether you do the commercial or not."

"Let's talk about it. I want you to be sure, okay? And your parents too."

"Okay," she says. "But you have to take that ridiculous cherry off your head. Fruit should be eaten, not worn as decorative headwear. Don't you know that?"

"What about the cupcake costume? Can I take that off?"

"No," she says. "Keep it on. I like it. It sold a lot of cupcakes today."

I smile through my tears. And then I reach out and hug her.

"Careful," she says. "I don't want to get frosting on my new shirt."

"I love you, Chickarita," I tell her.

"I love you too, Sophie Bird."

Dream #12—
I have the best friend
a girl could ever dream of.

Chapter 25

marshmallow chocolate-chip pie

OOEY, GOOEY PERFECTION

Christmas is wonderful. Dad loves his new robe, although he says he's keeping the old one as a memento of the good old days. Spit-up equals good old days? Okay, whatever. Mom is totally surprised by her box of tea, and proceeds to make herself a cup of it right away.

As for Hayden, I used my December allowance and got him three *Star Wars* figures, one of which is Yoda, his favorite character.

"Happy Jedi, I am," he says after he opens it. "Thank you."

Yes, we are now sharing a house with Yoda, which is about as much fun as wearing a cupcake costume in the pouring rain.

My haul includes new clothes, a bunch of new books, including *Bridge to Terabithia*, a gift certificate for an acting class, and my very own cell phone!

"Don't lose it" is the first thing my parents say to me after I open it.

Mom also got me a new purse, which has a special pocket inside specifically for the cell phone. And surprisingly enough, she did a good job picking out the purse. Although she went the easy route—she picked one that is almost identical to my old one. She's a smart one, my mother.

The day after Christmas, Mom drops me off at Isabel's house with my suitcase in hand. It's time to make the trek to Seattle, and I'm so excited!

Isabel takes me to her room and shows me all the cool stuff she got for Christmas—lots of cute clothes, an art set, a cute apron that says, "Top Chef," and a new suitcase.

"Wow, a suitcase, huh?" I ask her. "Does that mean there's a lot more traveling in your future?"

"I hope so," she says.

I help her finish packing, and then we head downstairs and wait for her parents in the cupcake shop. Her grandma is there, helping a couple of customers.

When she's finished, she says, "Hi, Sophie! So nice to see you! Ready to visit the Space Needle in the sky?"

"I'm ready!" I say. "It's going to be so much fun!"

"But don't forget," Isabel says. "First we have to stop and have pie at Penny's Pie Place."

I nudge Isabel and suddenly notice her hair looks really nice today. Like she spent a long time on it this morning. "Are you excited to see Jack?" I ask.

She smiles. "Maybe."

"Okay, girls," Isabel's mom says, peeking her head through the door. "We're ready to go. Thank you,

Mother, for holding down the fort while we're gone."

"You know I'm happy to do it. You guys have a wonderful time, all right?"

"We will," Isabel says. "Bye, Grandma!"

"Bye!"

Isabel and I pass the time in the car by playing cards with a deck she brought along and munching on Goldfish crackers and apples.

When we get to Seattle, it's blue skies and sunny, but cold. Perfect weather for going up in the Space Needle. The plan is to have some pie, and then we'll head over and spend the rest of the afternoon there.

The outside of the restaurant is bright yellow and red, and the words PENNY'S PIE PLACE are printed right on the building, above the awning. And next to the words is a big piece of apple pie on a yellow plate.

We go inside and a woman greets us. She's wearing a yellow dress with an apron. Her name tag says "Karen."

"Hello, can I help you?" she asks.

"I'm friends with Jack," Isabel tells her. "I told him we'd be coming this way today. Is he here?"

Just then, a cute boy with straight dark hair and

big brown eyes comes from around the corner. He smiles and shows his two dimples.

"Hey, Isabel," he says. He gives her a really quick hug, and then she introduces all of us to him.

"We're going to go sit down," Isabel's mom says. She looks at Isabel. "We know you want to catch up with your friend, so go ahead and get a table and order, okay?"

"Okay. Thanks, Mom."

Jack leads us over to a booth in the corner. I slide in one side of the booth, while Isabel slides in next to Jack.

"So, girls, welcome to Seattle," he says. "Otherwise known as the Emerald City. Unfortunately, we've given all of our emeralds away today, so all I have to give you is pie."

"Pie is good," Isabel says. "How many flavors do you have, anyway?"

"Twelve. But you have to trust me on this one, okay? Marshmallow chocolate-chip pie is the specialty pie this week, and I really think you should try it'"

"Marshmallow chocolate-chip pie?" I ask. "It sounds a little bit like a s'more."

"You're right!" he says. "It's actually the recipe I entered for the contest."

Both of our mouths drop open. "Really?" Isabel says. "I entered a s'more cupcake recipe. Well, until Mom sent in the recipe I really wanted to enter, which was for chocolate jam tarts."

Jack looks confused.

"Never mind," Isabel says. "Long story. The important thing is that it sounds delicious, and of course I want to try it!"

"Me too," I chime in.

Jack turns and looks at me. "Isabel told me in her last letter you're going to be in a commercial. You trying to put the rest of us out of business?"

I know he's joking, but it isn't very funny to me. It's still a sensitive topic, I guess.

Isabel smiles and says, "Sophie, maybe you could make a pie costume next. I bet people would love that. You'd sell hundreds of pies for them, I just know it."

I shout "No!" while Jack shouts "Yes!"

We laugh and then Jack's face gets all serious. "Actually," he says, leaning in and whispering, "just between us, Mom and Dad are thinking of closing the place down. Business hasn't been very good lately."

"Oh no," Isabel says as I feel my heart breaking in half.

"Is there anything we can do?" I ask.

"Nah, I don't think there's anything anyone can do. I mean, cupcakes are all the rage. They're cute, they're fun, and kids love them. Pies are sort of boring, you know?"

"I don't think so," I say. "I love pie."

"Do you love it more than cupcakes?" he asks.

I look at him. I look at Isabel. Then I throw my hands in the air. "Don't put me in another impossible situation! I've had my share, thank you very much."

They laugh at me, and then Karen comes to take our order and brings our slices of pie back a few minutes later.

"Oh my gosh, Jack," I say, "this is seriously the best pie I've *ever* had. Can I get the recipe?"

"Didn't Isabel tell you?" he whispers. "It's top-secret. If I told you, I'd have to kill you. But get me those secret brownie recipes and you might have a deal."

"That's it, Sophie!" Isabel squeals. "You can be

a spy for us. Find the secret to Beatrice's Brownie's success, and we can bring them down!"

"But I don't want to be a spy," I tell them. "I just want to be an actress. Is that too much to ask?" And with that, I throw my head down on the table and pretend to weep.

"She's good," I hear Jack say.

"You're telling me," Isabel says.

After we finish eating, I excuse myself to use the bathroom so Isabel can have a few minutes alone with Jack. I scrub my hands for a good five minutes, trying to drag out the inevitable. She's going to have to leave him, and I know she's not going to want to.

Finally, I walk out to find them standing by the front door with Isabel's parents, waiting on me.

"Bye, Jack," I say. "The pie was fabulous. Tell your parents I hope they can hang in there."

"Bye, Sophie. I will."

I head toward the car with Isabel's parents. Isabel stays behind a minute, saying good-bye to Jack in private.

When she finally gets in the car, she's beaming.

"To the Space Needle?" Isabel's dad asks.

"To the Space Needle!" we all shout back.

And as we drive away, Isabel opens her hand and shows me the silver necklace with the pink cupcake charm she's holding.

Awww. What a *sweet* guy.

Chapter 26

chocolate-dipped fortune cookie

IT SAYS YOUR FUTURE IS BRIGHT

For three days we have fun exploring Seattle. The Space Needle is really high. Like, amazingly high. I can't even go out on the viewing deck because it freaks me out.

We spend a whole afternoon shopping at Pike Place Market. We watch the men throw the fish over customers' heads and we eat all kinds of good food. We go to two museums, the Museum of Flight as well as the Science Fiction Museum. The whole time I'm there, I think of Hayden. He'd love it. He should *live* here!

And before I know it, we're driving back, heading toward Willow where school will be starting back up in just a few days.

Isabel is sad to be leaving, I can tell. She stayed happy through most of the trip, wearing the necklace he gave her the whole time, and reaching up to touch it every once in a while, like it made her feel close to him. But now we're heading home, and home is a long, long way from Seattle.

"Maybe he'll come visit you," I whisper.

"I hope so."

Isabel is writing stuff down in her little notebook, so I pull out my dream notebook and write:

Dream #13—
I dream of a happily ever after
for everyone.

❋ ❋ ❋

When I get home, Mom and Dad are glad to see me. Hayden says, "Good trip, was it?"

"Yes, a most excellent trip, Yoda wannabe. Mom, Dad, we have to take Hayden to the Science Fiction Museum someday. He would love it!"

"Maybe this summer," Dad says. "I haven't been to Seattle in a long time. It'd be fun to spend some time up there."

"Oh, and there's this great pie restaurant we have to go to." *If it stays open that long.* "Maybe I could bring Isabel with us, since she was nice enough to invite me to come with her."

"I don't see why not," Mom says.

Oh, wait until I tell Isabel! She'll be over-the-moon happy about the possibility of seeing Jack again.

At school I take Dennis Holt's movie back to him. I feel bad I had it for so long, but I kept forgetting to watch the ending. I finally found time last night. It was good, but sad, like everyone said. I definitely want to read the book now.

• *199* •

I find Dennis at his locker before school starts.

When he turns around, I can't believe what I see. Is this really him?

"Dennis, what . . . what happened?"

"I got contacts. And I finally listened to my mom and got my hair cut. I'm not sure about it. What do you think?"

"I think it looks fantastic." As soon as I say it, I feel my cheeks getting warm.

"Well, thanks," he says. "If you like it, then it must be all right."

We chat for a while, about Christmas and stuff, and then the warning bell rings, telling us it's time to head to class.

"Oh, wait, I almost forgot. I brought your movie back. Thanks for letting me borrow it. It was really good."

"You're welcome," he says as he throws the movie into his locker and shuts the door. "Someday I bet I'll be watching you in a movie like that."

I shrug. "Maybe. We'll see what people have to say about the commercial first."

"Yeah, when do we get to watch it?" he asks.

"We shot the commercial last week, when I got back from Seattle. They're saying it will air for the first time in a couple of weeks. I'm so nervous!"

"It'll be great," he says. "That reminds me, I have something for you, too. I'm not sure what you're going to think, but uh, well, I want to give it to you."

He stops and rummages around in that messy binder of his, and pulls out something in a plastic wrapper. He hands it to me and says, "I hope it's not broken."

I look at it closely and see it's a chocolate-dipped fortune cookie with sprinkles on the outside. And it isn't broken. It's really pretty. Almost too pretty to eat.

"A fortune cookie?" I ask.

"Yeah," he says. "My way of saying congratulations on the commercial. Open it!"

I take off the plastic wrap, and break the cookie open to read the fortune.

It says: "In the shadowy light of the stronghold everything seemed possible."—From *Bridge to Terabithia* (Remember—everything is possible!)

Aw. What a *sweet* guy!

"Thanks, Dennis. I love it." I hand him a piece of the cookie, and we eat as we walk to class. When we get there, he stops just outside the doorway.

"I almost forgot to tell you," he says. "I got the best camera for Christmas. My mom said a little elf helped her pick it out. Do you know anything about that?"

I try to look shocked. "No! Why would you think that?"

He smiles. "I don't know. Just a guess. Hey, Austen and I are going to enter a photography contest. Grand prize is five hundred bucks! What do you think? You in?"

I laugh. "No, thanks. No more contests for me for a while."

"Okay, well, maybe you can help me with mine."

"As long as it doesn't involve dead birds or gutted fish, I'll help you."

And then, he leans in a little bit. "Sophie, do you know how I said one time I wished you were a boy?"

"Yes."

"I just want you to know, I think I've changed my mind on that."

As I walk to my desk I feel my heart beating really

hard. Almost as hard as the moment I found out Mom was taking me to see *Wicked*.

Does this mean I like Dennis Holt almost as much as I like musicals?

Oh. My. Gosh.

I think it does!

Chocolate Jam Tarts

2 ⅔ cups flour

I cup butter, chilled

⅓ cup unsweetened cocoa

4 tablespoons sugar

½ teaspoon baking powder

I egg yolk

⅓ cup ice-cold water

½ cup strawberry jam

Preheat oven to 400°. Blend flour and butter together using butter knives and/or a pastry blender until butter is marble size. Stir in cocoa. Make a well and add the sugar, baking powder, egg yolk, and water. Quickly combine all ingredients. Use hands to knead the dough into a ball, then place on a floured surface and roll to ¼-inch thickness.

Using a butter knife, cut into 3-inch squares. Put a tablespoonful of jam in the center of each square, fold into a triangle, and crimp the edges together.

Place on a greased baking sheet and bake for 10

minutes. Cool for 30 minutes and sift powdered sugar over the top of the tarts.

Monster Cookies

1 cup brown sugar

1 cup granulated sugar

½ cup butter or margarine

1 ½ cups creamy peanut butter

3 eggs

1 teaspoon vanilla

1 tablespoon Karo syrup

4 ½ cups rolled oats

½ cup flour

2 teaspoons baking soda

1 cup M&M's

1 cup chocolate chips

With a mixer, beat together sugars, butter, and peanut butter. Add the eggs, vanilla, and Karo syrup, and mix well. Gradually add in the rolled oats, flour, and baking soda, and mix until well blended. Stir in the M&M's and chocolate chips. Refrigerate dough for at least 3 hours (can even be overnight) to help cookies mound up better. When ready to bake, preheat oven to 350°, and use a teaspoon to drop onto ungreased baking sheets. Bake about 12 minutes, until a light golden brown.

acknowledgments

First and foremost I have to thank all of the kids who wrote to me, letting me know how much they enjoyed the book *It's Raining Cupcakes*. It's because of *you* that I decided to write another book about Isabel and Sophie. I hope you find this book just as sweet!

Deena Lipomi, you helped me come up with the premise, so I'm not sure this book would exist without you! Thanks also to Kate, Emily, and Tina for helping to brainstorm ideas.

Lindsey and Lisa, you thought long and hard on titles, so I have to say thanks for that. Triple Ls, always and forever.

I want to send a big thank-you out to Allie Costa and Amanda Morgan, who answered my questions about commercial auditions and provided valuable feedback on an important part of the book.

Thank you to my editor, Alyson, and all of the fine people at Aladdin who helped bake this book into something that's not only pretty to look at but also delicious to read.

Thanks, as always, to my agent, Sara.

Thank you, Katherine Paterson, for writing *Bridge to Terabithia*, one of the greatest books of all time.

When I needed to brainstorm funny things boys would say, I turned to my husband, Scott, who is an expert at being funny. I like funny boys, and I'm glad I'm married to one.

My kids have to put up with many dinner conversations that start out, "I need some help with . . ." Thanks, boys, for not only putting up with me but also for being the best kids a mom could ask for. I want to say something really mushy, but I'll refrain. You're welcome.